LOVE KILLS

Stella Grossman
> loved a younger man—and lost an older man's money.

Arthur Coppock
> loved the Grossman inheritance—and where there's a will there's a way.

Helga Grossman
> loved like a sister—and something more.

Philip Sutton
> loved women, men, and, most of all, a good swindle.

Terry Jenkins
> loved attention—and got more than he asked for.

They all loved Carl Grossman. One of them was his killer.

And it's up to Kate and Henry Theobald—today's answer to Lord Peter and Harriet Vane—to unravel an exceedingly tangled web of love and murder.

DEATH by HOAX
LIONEL BLACK

AVON
PUBLISHERS OF BARD, CAMELOT AND DISCUS BOOKS

AVON BOOKS
A division of
The Hearst Corporation
959 Eighth Avenue
New York, New York 10019

First Avon Printing, December, 1978

AVON TRADEMARK REG. U.S. PAT. OFF. AND IN
OTHER COUNTRIES, MARCA REGISTRADA, HECHO IN
U.S.A.

Printed in the U.S.A.

DEATH BY HOAX

CHAPTER 1

CHAPTER 1

It was the silly season, and hot even for August.

Butch beckoned Kate Theobald over to the news desk. "It's the silly season."

Kate eyed him warily. "What's on your mind?"

"Loxham Bay. Know it?"

"Grotty little seaside town on the south coast, all oil on the beaches, and kiss-me-quick hats, and hot dogs and winkles. Oh no, Butch. Please."

"We've got a stringer there, young fellow named Geoff Hayward. He can't write at all, but he has good ideas. He's just phoned in this piece about a hoaxer."

"Hoaxer?"

"There's an outbreak of hoaxes in the town. False alarms calling out the fire brigade, doctors being got out at midnight to non-existent car smashes—that sort of thing."

"So we work it up, and start several more moronic teenagers calling out the fire brigade and weary doctors."

Butch shrugged. "Come off it, Kate. We're a newspaper, not a social service. The place is only a couple of hours by train. Have a look at it. If you think there's nothing in it, come back today. I'll call the stringer and tell him to meet you at the station."

She did not enjoy the journey. The carriage was crammed with perspiring mothers, and excited kids rushing up and down the aisle shouting and hitting each other. After a couple of pages, she left her book listlessly on her lap; too hot to read. She stared through the grubby windowpane at the interminable little houses of the London suburbs. But then at last came fields, hills, coppices, a machine leisurely cutting and stacking hay, cows grazing on the lush bank of a stream, farmhouses, sedentary sheep. Kate sighed. On such a day to be pursuing a silly-season story!

Towards the end of the journey she re-read the piece the stringer had phoned. He had written it so ham-fistedly that she began to realize it seemed duller than it might turn out to be. In not much more than three weeks some asinine joker had pulled off five hoaxes. She counted them. Geoff Hayward hadn't had the sense to bring that point out.

A couple had been fairly alarming. A mid-evening call to the police warned there was a bomb in the town's only movie theatre. As the audience was got out in a hurry, an elderly woman stumbled, fell and was trampled on. If two men hadn't linked arms across the exit door, and held the rush while the theatre manager calmed everybody, there might have been panic. There was, of course, no bomb.

Three days later a phone caller reported that a man had been seen to enter the railway tunnel through the hill to the north of the town. All trains were halted and the current switched off while a couple of railwaymen searched the tunnel. Nobody there. But the train service was held up for three hours. Also, because of some freak connection of the main electricity supply, it had to be cut off from the industrial estate bordering the railway line, and half a dozen factories lost three hours' production. Worst hit was an electronics factory, the biggest single employer of labour in the town, which was on full overtime to complete a rush export order.

Kate pondered. What was happening in a small town where some anonymous imbecile was making that kind of mischief? Nerves starting to crack? Could be—especially in this heat. Tempers rising? Even signs of mass hysteria? The stringer had missed all that. There might be more to the story than she had at first imagined.

CHAPTER 2

Maybe the young man waiting for her at the station was
no literary genius, but he was tall, broad, tough-looking,
handsome. Kate smiled approval. "I'm Kate Theobald."

"Gosh, it's nice meeting you. I never thought the
Post'd send their star on this little story."

Kate smiled modestly. "It's the silly season. Now,
where do we start?"

He had assumed that she would want to talk first to
the police, so he had lined up his best contact, Sergeant
Pace. Just about now, he told her as he led to his elderly,
somewhat rusted car parked in the station yard, Bob Pace
would be in the snug at the Fishermen's Rest. "Nice little
pub in the Old Town, close to the back door to the police
station."

He drove with such abandon that Kate managed only
a sidelong glance at the town. She was nervously occupied watching the road. She was aware of the usual small-
town shopping streets, coloured lights strung between the
lampposts of the esplanade, refreshment stalls, sunbathing crowds stretched out on the beach, children paddling
in the shallows, swimmers beyond, and at one end a
harbour wall of weathered stone sheltering half a dozen
fishing vessels, a few sailing craft and a huddle of ding-
hies.

A curiosity of Geoff Hayward's car, she noted, was
that to drop from top to second gear he had to thrust
with brute strength at the old-style gear lever on the floor.
Every time, down came his heavy fist, slamming the lever
with a grinding roar, though seemingly with only a twist

of his broad shoulder. Certainly a football player, Kate
thought approvingly, probably a boxer.

"Bob Pace is a friend of mine," he told her as he
swerved into the steep, narrow streets of the Old Town.
"He's most co-operative. He'll always slip me the facts,
on the quiet. I did him a good turn once, in the local
sheet."

The Fishermen's Rest, half-timbered, white rendering,
diamond-pane lattices sloping with age, was terraced between two similar, genuinely Tudor houses. Sergeant
Pace was the only man in the snug, standing up to the
small bar with a pint tankard in his hand. He was in
civilian clothes, grey trousers, open-neck shirt; his face
round, rubicund; the tips of his moustaches waxed, like
those of an Army drill instructor.

Geoff introduced them and got drinks. Another pint
for the sergeant. Same for Geoff himself. And what would
Kate take? Something long and cool. Cold lager? Lovely,
she agreed, settling on a bar stool to drink it slowly.

"She's down here from the *Post* to write about our
hoaxes," said Geoff.

"There's been another," the sergeant told him. "It's on
now. Grossman Electronics had a phone call this morning to say there's a bomb on their premises."

"Getting a bit repetitive," suggested Kate, "another
bomb scare?"

The sergeant reckoned it was the Irish troubles started
the whole thing off. Stood to reason. All that bombing.
Some half-witted youth gets fascinated. The sergeant was
surprised there hadn't been a lot more of it all over the
place, and surprised it was as harmless as a hoax. Some
day some crazy teenager without any political motive
would set off an actual bomb just for fun. That sort of
thing spread like a grass fire.

Where would they get the explosives? Oh, that wasn't
difficult. Quarries never kept proper checks on their explosive stocks. Lots of it got stolen, some for safe-blow-
ers, and some, the sergeant reckoned, for wherever the

latest bunch of murdering bastards was raising hell. The world had gone crazy.

Kate asked if it was worrying the local townsfolk much. Starting to, the sergeant admitted. People were going out less at night. The theatre owner was moaning it would ruin him, and the pubs were suffering, even though they had the holiday trade. Some of the small hotels reported visitors cancelling after a few days and going off home.

Then there was a stream of calls from old ladies after dark, swearing there were intruders in their gardens.

"We have to divert a car, and there never is an intruder. But the old dears have to be calmed down. The time it takes! Like all police forces, we're undermanned. And this on top of everything! It's lucky we don't get much serious crime here—mostly small break-ins, or drunken brawls, or indecent exposures—that sort of thing. Because if a professional lot moved in here, they'd find the police almost too worn-out to cope. It's driving us round the twist."

"Have Grossman's stopped work?" asked Geoff.

"They don't know what to do. There isn't a bomb, of course. But dare a management risk it? To make it worse, Carl Grossman is away on a business trip. In his absence, Arthur Coppock can't make up his mind whether to evacuate the place or not. We've got a few chaps up there, searching. They'll find nothing."

"This is the third time Grossman's have had it," Geoff told Kate. "They're the biggest factory on the industrial estate that was shut down by the scare of a man in the railway tunnel. Then a couple of days ago a man telephoned to say that a poisonous irritant had been slipped into the plastic containers of a chemical paste the women use on the assembly benches."

"I read that in your story, but didn't realize it was the same factory."

"Yes, Grossman Electronics. Carl Grossman had the stuff analysed—did the job himself, I've heard. They've got a small chemistry lab. And, of course, it was okay.

But he had lost a half-day's work on the benches, and a lot of the women weren't quite convinced, and their speed suffered, and a few even turned it up and went home."

Kate asked the policeman, "Has anybody else been affected more than once?"

Sergeant Pace thought carefully, then said he reckoned not.

"We should have a look at this factory, Geoff," she suggested.

"Okay. One more drink first." To the barman, "Same again."

Driving through the town, Geoff gave her a rundown on Grossman Electronics. The biggest local employer of skilled labour—of any labour, probably. It made electronic components, some of them highly specialized for computers and calculators. But mostly its products were components for industrial machines, timing devices, automatic switchgear, control circuits.

"Tell me about the boss."

"Carl Grossman. He's the scientist. He invented quite a lot of the stuff the factory produces. Originally he was German—and Jewish, I suppose. He came here in 1939 as a refugee from Hitler. The Nazis were daft to let him go. He was still a young man, but already a highly-qualified scientist, and a bit of a genius. We used him during the war on secret technical work, and I've heard said he was worth a squadron of fighters. He was on aircraft detection techniques, especially night-fighters. In 1946 he started up his own firm in a very small way, in a store shed down by the harbour here. Now he has built it into an international business, particularly during the last few years. Grossman components now go all over the world. I think he made parts for some of the instruments used in American spacecraft."

"Is the firm still on defence work?"

"I imagine so, though of course that doesn't get talked about. I don't know if there's any specially secret part of the factory, but the whole building's under a pretty good security guard, which makes it even less necessary than usual to pay attention to the hoaxer."

"Who's Arthur Coppock?"

"The managing director. He's primarily an accountant —nice chap, local, sits on the Council, used to play for the best rugger club in town, but he's too old for that now. I suppose he must be in his fifties. My father has known him for years, and of course I know him quite well. He runs the business side. Grossman leaves all that to him. Arthur joined up with Grossman only about a year after he started the firm. They work together as a good team, Arthur says."

He swerved the car suddenly across an intersection into a side road, just beating the lights.

"The industrial estate's along here, on the borders of the town. There's almost no other local industry, except the hotel and holiday trade and a small inshore fishing fleet."

The road opened on to a complex of factories, warehouses, loading bays, car and truck parks, a railway siding. Geoff ran his car towards the biggest building in a large fenced enclosure. The guard at the gate recognized him and waved him through.

In the main office Geoff approached a smart-looking redhead. "Morning, Vera. Mr. Grossman back yet?"

"Not yet. He's been recalled and he's driving down from London."

"Could I have a word with Mr. Coppock then? This is Kate Theobald, the *Post*'s best writer. She's come to write about our hoaxer."

Vera smiled wryly. "It doesn't seem quite so funny this morning. I'll ask." She spoke into the phone, then nodded. "All right. You know the way. But he says to be brief. He's got one hell of a load until Mr. Grossman gets here."

"Sure," said Geoff, leading Kate towards the lift.

Arthur Coppock exactly fitted the image she had formed from Geoff's brief rundown: thickset, of moderate height, his light-coloured hair thinning, wearing

spectacles which he pulled off his face when he looked
up from his desk. Then she saw how alert his pale blue
eyes were, and noticed the sharpness of his thin nose.
The jacket of his tweed suit, much too thick for such
weather, hung from a hatstand behind him. The papers
on his desk were meticulously arranged, nothing out of
place.

Geoff introduced Kate. "She's here to write about our
hoaxer."

"I wish you wouldn't," said Coppock. "Publicity will
only make it worse. That sort of disease is catching."

"I sympathize, Mr. Coppock. But a newspaper's job
is to report what happens. Here, this morning, for instance."

"The point, after all, is that nothing is really happening. Soon after the place opened, a man phoned to say
there's a bomb in the factory. That's all. It's a non-event."

"Who took the call?"

"One of the girls in the office."

"Vera Sanderson," said Geoff. "The redhead. You
just met her."

"Talk to her if you wish," offered Coppock. "But that's
all she can tell you. A crazy man on the phone, then he
rings off."

"What sort of voice?"

"I don't know. Ask Vera." The house phone rang on
his desk. "Hallo . . . Oh good. By the way, the young
woman from the *Post* wants to know what sort of voice
telephoned you this morning . . . Okay, I'll tell her." He
replaced the phone. "That was Vera. She says she can't
tell what sort of voice. It was muffled. He was probably
talking through a scarf or a handkerchief. She could only
just make out the words. And, thank heavens, Carl
Grossman is back. She rang to say his car was turning
in through the gates. Now he can take over."

"You feel certain there isn't really a bomb?" asked
Kate.

"Of course. It's just some joker getting a kick out of

making trouble. Somebody deprived, I'd say, and this is his taste of power."

Kate agreed. "But if you're sure, why close the works?"

"I haven't closed them. The police are looking through some of the shops, and a few of the women have got nervous and gone out into the yard."

The office door was pushed open and a small, dapper, slightly swarthy man came in, a wallet under his arm. He glanced sharply at the visitors, then said quietly to Coppock, "Tell me." His voice, Kate thought, was more agreeable than his appearance. He looked a hard, arrogant, ruthless little man. But his voice was soft, almost caressing.

"Another hoax," Coppock told him. "The joker rang just after the works opened and said there's a bomb in the building. Didn't say where. Vera took the call. Before she could get him talking, in the hope that somebody could get the police on another line, he hung up. Then she rang me at home, but I was already on my way in."

"What have you done?"

"Called the police, of course, as soon I got here. I asked the sergeant if I ought to evacuate the place. He said that, officially, he was bound to advise me to do so, just in case. But it was up to me. I made a little speech on the PA circuit, telling everybody it was just another stupid hoax, and the police were there as a matter of routine. Most of them accepted that, but some of the women have come off the assembly line. Production is badly cut. Perhaps you can persuade them to go back."

"It would be better for the police to assure them that there's no danger."

"Doubt if they will," murmured Coppock.

"Ask the sergeant to step up to my office."

As he turned to leave, Kate said, "I'm from the *Post*, Mr. Grossman. I'm to write something about this hoax business. I'd appreciate a word with you."

Grossman halted. "There's nothing I can tell you. You see for yourself what the situation is."

He turned abruptly and went out.

Coppock picked up his house phone. "Vera, get some-body to find the police sergeant and ask him to go up to Mr. Grossman's office. Yes, Mr. Grossman has gone to his office now. And, Vera, the young woman from the *Post* wants to ask you a few questions about the phone call this morning. What's that? Oh yes, tell her anything you can. I've warned her it isn't much."

He got up from his chair and held out his hand.

"Now I must ask you to leave. There really is nothing more I can tell you."

Kate took his hand. It was damp with sweat, rather unpleasant. Any man who wore a thick tweed suit in this weather . . .

"Thank you for your help."

Coppock said to Geoff, "Sorry I can't do more. But you can see for yourself what the situation is. Nothing is happening here that you don't already know."

The sudden thud of an explosion shook the window frames, rattled the desk, the chairs. In the moment of intense silence that followed, the three stared at each other, frozen into stillness. Then, as tumult broke out below, they rushed to the open window.

Black smoke was gushing from a window on the same level, a short distance along the wall.

Coppock cried, "Good God! Carl's office."

He turned and ran from the room, along the corridor, Kate and Geoff close behind him. Smoke was billowing through the broken glass panel of the second door. Peo-ple were standing, aghast, at the far end of the corridor. Kate was dimly aware of the sound of others running up from below.

Coppock thrust open the door. Then recoiled.

Kate shoved herself alongside him, stuffing her hand-kerchief across her mouth and nose to filter the acrid smoke.

But it was pouring out of the window fast enough to clear vision in the room. The top of the huge desk was ripped open, glass shattered, papers burning, woodwork flickering with flame. Lamps, chairs, bookcases, broken and overthrown.

The desk chair itself had been blown back against the wall, and toppled. Sprawled across it, blackened, lay what remained of Carl Grossman. Face sliced off. One arm pulped. Chest torn open, blood pouring out, a scarlet froth spreading across the blackness of the burned clothes, the flesh.

Kate turned away, wanting to vomit. Past her went running the firemen with a foam extinguisher smothering the smouldering desk; a couple of men racing towards Grossman's body, then standing irresolute, horrified; the factory nurse running in, halting, choking a scream, then turning, stumbling away, nothing she could do.

Kate got out somehow into the corridor, now crowded. She saw Geoff bringing out Coppock, almost carrying him. Coppock's face was ceiling white, he was shuddering like a man with palsy, and small, protesting moans were coming from his throat. Geoff, looking quickly to see that Kate was all right, began to elbow a way through the people in the corridor, supporting Coppock towards his own office, calling to the nurse to follow.

CHAPTER 3

From her balcony on the Royal Albert Hotel Kate gazed across the esplanade and the beach littered with holiday-makers at the placid water of the bay, sipping at the same time a large gin and tonic. To steady her nerves, she told Geoff. And she could soon do with another. She approved, she added, of the rooms Geoff had quickly booked for her—the Royal Albert's only suite, of sitting-room, bathroom and double bedroom, since Henry would soon be coming to join her. The Royal Albert, Geoff had told her, was just about the only reasonable hotel in the place; a pile of solid Victorian red brick, massively, if rather shabbily, furnished. Dickens had once stayed there, Geoff had told her, which was why his rooms were labelled the Pickwick Suite; though, of course, it was not *Pickwick* that Dickens was supposed to have written there, but part of *Little Dorritt,* Geoff believed, or maybe *Great Expectations*.

Never mind the literary associations, Kate had in-structed, but grab the suite. By nightfall, when the rest of Fleet Street got to Loxham Bay, there wouldn't be a vacant hotel room in the town.

The news agencies would have picked up the facts of the explosion by now, but nobody could get the firsthand story she had already phoned to the *Post*. When she was switched to the news desk, Butch had crowed.

"Stay on it, girl, hard as you can. Do you want any help? I'll send a couple of reporters."

"No, I'm all right on my own. But ring Henry and ask him to bring the car down. He may be at his chambers, but it's vacation, so he'll probably be either at his club or at home in Chelsea."

"What's the angle? How do you see it so far?"

"It must be murder, quite deliberate and carefully planned. The bomb was in the drawer of the man's desk, and the drawer was locked—anyway, seems to have been. It looks as though it was triggered off when he unlocked it."

"Then what's the significance of the previous hoaxes?"

"Butch, dear, your guess is probably better than mine."

"What's Grossman's background?"

"Give me a chance to get my breath back," Kate had told him, "and to still my girlish tremors, and I'll start to find out."

So where to start.

"Was Grossman married?" she asked Geoff as he came out on to the balcony with the second gins.

"Yes, twice. His first wife, Phyllis, was a girl he met during the war. She was in one of the women's services. She died about ten years ago. His second wife's name is Stella. She's a lot younger than Grossman, who must have been in his fifties. I doubt if Stella is yet forty. She's a bit of all right—classical sort of looks, but rather sulky, damn nice figure, long dark hair in a bun at the back of her neck. She looks like a ballet dancer, but in fact she's a musician, a violinist. I don't know much about her, where she came from or anything. It was probably music that introduced her to Grossman."

"He was musical?"

"Mad on it. My father says mathematical scientists often are. Grossman was a good musician. He played the viola in his string quartet."

"His own?"

"Only amateur. They played at his house every Tuesday and Saturday evenings. Stella was the first violin. Tuesdays were private. I suppose they were practising. On Saturdays, groups of local people were invited as an audience. I had to go once, with my family. Do you know anything more boring than chamber music?"

Kate laughed. "And the house?"

"It's a lovely old place, a couple of miles outside the town, on the bank of the river. Warnham Court. It's pretty big, and stands in about twenty acres, mostly ornamental, though he did run a few sheep. Must have cost a mint to keep up. But Carl Grossman's a rich man—or rather, was."

Kate downed the rest of her gin.

"All right, Geoff. Before the other hounds get here, let's go to Warnham Court."

Certainly a lovely old place, Kate agreed, when Geoff turned his antique car through the wrought-iron gateway of the drive and pulled up on the wide circle of gravel before the house. The front was classic Georgian, big sash windows, pillars on either side of a charmingly fanlighted front door. But the lower part of the house at the rear looked older, probably Elizabethan that had been built on to. Through thick shrubs to one side she could just make out a lawn, then white railings and, beyond, a stretch of grassland dotted with trees running down to a distant gleam that must be the river.

Two police cars were already drawn up to one side of the circle, the drivers leaning on one of the bonnets, chatting. One of them came over to Geoff's car, recognized him, nodded. Kate brought out her union card, at which the constable glanced, checking the photo.

"You can't see Mrs. Grossman now. She's with the Super."

"Wouldn't want to intrude on private grief anyhow," Kate told him. "But maybe there's somebody else in the house we could see. No harm in asking."

Looking doubtful, the constable let them pass.

The front door was opened by a young man—early twenties, Kate reckoned. His hair was fashionably long, his clothes were fashionably shabby.

"Yes? Oh, it's you, Geoff."

Geoff introduced him. "Philip Sutton. We were at school together. This is Kate Theobald from the *Post*."

The young man's interest quickened at that, Kate thought. The usual vanity—name in the newspapers. He wasn't bad-looking. Cleaned up a bit, he'd have been quite presentable.

"Philip's a musician," Geoff went on. "He studied in London."

"And in Paris."

"He's a violinist. He plays in the string quartet. Or rather . . ." He broke off awkwardly, then asked, "What's happening, Phil?"

"Nothing much. What can happen here? It's at the factory."

It occurred to Kate that the second violin of the Grossman string quartet was not unduly upset by the death of the viola. But perhaps, she quickly told herself, that was only her fancy.

"Stella's been shut up in the music room for half an hour with a couple of policemen," said Philip Sutton. "What they're talking about, heaven knows. How can Stella know anything about it? Arthur Coppock sent me here to break the news. It was actually a bomb."

Kate nodded. "In the locked drawer of Mr. Grossman's desk."

"You know?" he asked, astonished.

"We were in the room," Geoff told him, "a few seconds after it happened."

"Was it awful?"

"Gruesome. How is Mrs. Grossman taking it?"

"Bit too calm, if you ask me."

"You work at the factory?" inquired Kate.

"In the office."

A door opened at the far side of the large, octagonal hall, exquisitely furnished, Kate saw, and with a huge, magnificent vase of flowers on a pedestal. A man came across the hall towards the front door. As he neared, Kate recognized him: Detective-Inspector Sam Kippis. At the same time he recognized her.

"Mrs. Theobald, isn't it?" he smiled wryly. "Mr. Wake will be delighted."

"Detective Chief Superintendent Roger Wake," explained Geoff helpfully.

"We have met," Kate told him. "Once before I covered a murder case Mr. Wake was handling."

The inspector suddenly laughed. "Covered it? You damn nearly swamped it." To Philip Sutton he added, "I'd rather you didn't say anything to the newspapers, Mr. Sutton, until the superintendent has had a word with you."

"Mr. Wake will want a word with me too, I expect," said Kate. "My colleague and I were first on the spot when the bomb exploded."

Kippis stared grimly at her. "I know. I've seen the statements you made to the sergeant who was on the premises when the bomb exploded."

"It was all done in such a rush," said Kate. "We might easily have left out something vital. I really think Mr. Wake will want to go over it again with us. After all, we were talking to Mr. Coppock—and to Mr. Grossman too —in Mr. Coppock's office. Then Mr. Grossman went to his own office, and soon after came the explosion. We were there, with Mr. Coppock, within seconds."

Sam Kippis gazed at her for a moment, then muttered, "Dear lord in heaven!," turned, and went out to one of the police cars.

"Mr. Wake and Inspector Kippis," Kate demurely explained to Philip Sutton, "are not all that fond of the Press."

One of the police cars started up and drove round to the front door. Across the hall came Roger Wake. He hadn't changed much, thought Kate—tall, lean, slightly hunched shoulders, unsmiling face. He looked hard at Kate as he passed, but said nothing, and got into the car. He was quickly driven away, followed by Kippis in the second car.

From inside the house a woman's voice asked, "Who are you talking to, Philip?"

"Reporters from the *Daily Post*."

Stella Grossman came towards them. She not only

looked like a dancer, Kate thought, but moved like one. Lovely creature, feline.

"Mrs. Grossman," Kate said, "the last thing we want to do is to intrude on you at such a time. Please don't think I was asking to see you."

"Well, now you have seen me, what do you want?"

Kate understood what Philip Sutton had meant when he said she was taking it a bit too calmly. Grief suppressed as rigidly as that must end in breakdown. Unless, of course, Kate thought, there was not much grief. It might be worth finding out how husband and wife had got along.

"If you really don't mind, there are a couple of questions."

"Well?"

"What happened must have been deliberately planned to kill your husband. Is there anybody you think might have done such a ghastly thing? He would not only have to have hated Mr. Grossman, but also been half crazy."

The woman slowly shook her head. "I know of nobody."

"The second question is whether he had given open support to Israel. He was, I believe, Jewish. Was he a likely target for the Palestinian terrorists—the letter-bomb thing?"

Again Stella Grossman shook her head. "Carl wasn't Jewish, either by race, or, certainly, by religion."

"A refugee from the Nazis," murmured Kate.

"I think he had a little Jewish blood—one great-grandfather or something. But he fled from Germany because he was a radical."

"So, nothing to do with Israel, or Arab terrorists?"

"Nothing. And now, if you'll excuse me . . ."

"Of course. I'm most grateful to you for seeing me at such a time. And may I say how sad I am that you have suffered such a loss?"

"Thank you," said the woman, turning away.

As they drove back to the hotel Kate said to Geoff,

"I suppose Philip Sutton was sent to break the news be-cause he plays in the string quartet, a friend."

"Yes," agreed Geoff, and then, after hesitation, "partly."

"You mean that he and Stella Grossman . . . ?"

"There has been some gossip."

"Must have been rather more than gossip if Coppock chooses Sutton to go to the house with the news."

"Oh well, Arthur's an old friend of Carl and Stella. He must have known."

"And did Carl Grossman know too? Was there any sort of crisis—divorce threatened or anything?"

"Not that I ever heard," said Geoff.

CHAPTER 4

At the Royal Albert, Henry Theobald was already unpacking in the Pickwick Suite.

Kate kissed him. "Thanks for coming, darling. This is Geoff Hayward, the *Post* man for this area. Geoff, this is my husband Henry. Nothing to do with newspapers. He's a lawyer—a barrister. And he has the most useful legal mind. Logic is Henry's thing. Darling, you came in the car?"

"Yes."

Kate giggled with relief. "Geoff is a dear, and a great help, and a pleasure to work with. He knows everybody hereabouts, and everything that goes on, and you can see for yourself how handsome he is. But he has the most dangerous antique of a car I've ever trembled to sit in, and he drives like an un-breathalysed maniac."

Geoff grinned. "It's a perfectly good car. I bought it for £75 and rebuilt the engine myself."

"Next," murmured Kate, "you should work on the steering—and the brakes."

"You were wise to grab these rooms, Kate," said Henry. "The newspapermen have already converged on the town. I passed several I recognized on the road."

"Henry drives a Jag he got cheap from a client he defended," explained Kate to Geoff. "The client isn't going to need it for at least three years, even if he gets full remission for good conduct."

"You can't win every time," said Henry. "And it wasn't all that cheap—more than seventy-five quid, anyhow. And I've extended your booking of the rooms for a second week, so that nobody else can grab them and chuck us out."

"What did I tell you?" said Kate admiringly to Geoff. "The trained mind, thinks of everything, solves every problem. Let's go and sit on the balcony in the sunshine and see what you make of this one, Henry darling. Geoff, ring down and ask them to send some tea."

When they were settled on the balcony, sipping the tea, Kate gazed at the beach, the bathers, the pier, and an elderly paddle-steamer tying up alongside it. "Not exactly St. Tropez, but there could be worse settings for a murder story in the heat of summer. I bet that steamer's got a brass plaque on the bridge saying it was one of the rescue fleet that went to Dunkirk."

"Very likely," Henry agreed. "Now then, the problem."

Kate gave in detail an account of all that had happened, all that she knew; only the facts, none of her guesses. "Well?"

Henry considered. "Seems to me there are two questions that need to be answered before one can get very far."

"Question number one."

"Why the hoaxes? Why should somebody who is going to commit a carefully-planned murder lead up to it with a series of false alarms?"

"Any possible answer?"

"Not yet. Not enough facts. Probably the only way is to find every known detail of the previous hoaxes—how many of them did you say?"

"Five," said Geoff.

"Well then, Geoff," Henry asked, "would you write down everything you know about each of the earlier hoaxes, and add any more details you can get from your local sources? Then we'll study the result. There has to be a pattern. The difficulty will be seeing it."

"I'll do that, straight away, this afternoon."

"The second question," continued Henry, "must be about motive. The question is, was Carl Grossman killed for reasons connected with his private life, or with his business?"

"Sex or greed?" put in Kate.

"Probably—though there could be other motivations. But you're probably right. Sex or greed?"

Geoff got up to go. "I'll have a talk with Bob Pace and check the details of the previous hoaxes."

Kate poured another cup of tea for her husband. "Now, which alternative do you fancy?"

"Neither as yet. All we have on 'sex' is gossip that Grossman's wife is having it off with young Philip Sutton, the second violin, and Arthur Coppock probably knew about it. Even if the gossip is true, we don't know whether Carl Grossman knew about it too. As for 'greed,' we really haven't any facts at all yet. But when Butch rang me, I asked him to get a report on Grossman Electronics from the *Post*'s business editor and phone it through here."

"How will that help?"

"If it's a public company, quoted on the Stock Exchange, a great deal will be known publicly about its financial situation. But if it's a private company, which I expect, very little will be published. But the financial chap on the *Post* will probably know quite a lot, especially if there are any rumours going round in the City."

"Evidence of greed? The firm's a bit groggy, so somebody murders the Chairman? It doesn't sound all that likely to me."

Henry laughed. "An over-simplification, wouldn't you say?"

"I wouldn't know. You're the financial brain, darling. You sit here and think about it." She got up. "I'm going to take a bath."

She was coming out of the bathroom, wrapped in her dressing-gown, when the phone rang. She picked it up.

"It's Butch," she called to Henry. "He's got the financial report you wanted." Into the phone she said, "I've got a bit more, Butch. I've interviewed the wife. All negative, but we can quote her to show that I got to her, and I bet nobody else does. The police are clamping down quite firmly. It's our old friend Roger Wake. Yes, dandy, ain't it? Why do you always pick on this county for my assignments? However, I'll file later. There's bound to be a Press conference of some sort this evening. Now I'll pass you over to Henry."

While he was at the phone she saw that it was nearly six o'clock, and poured herself a gin and tonic, and a scotch and soda for him, handing it to him while he listened; he raised his eyebrows in silent gratitude.

Kate wandered out on to the balcony. The sun was dropping towards the western headland, the evening light starting to spread over the sea. Fascinating the seashore is, she lazily mused, even in a small holiday resort like this. The kids were being marched off the beach, several of them yelling, towards high tea in their boarding-houses. Buckets and spades downed for the day. Boys were starting to parade slowly along the esplanade, staring at a few couples of girls, preparatory to pick-ups. A plodding attendant in peaked cap and overalls was collecting and stacking the hired deckchairs left scattered over the beach.

Henry came out beside her, a paper of notes in his hand.

"As I thought, it's a private company. It's heavily backed by a merchant bank in the City. But there's absolutely nothing known to suggest any trouble. The *Post* says it was a small firm until a few years ago, when it pulled off some big contracts. Since then, it is reputed to have expanded very fast, and Grossman would almost certainly have been a paper millionaire if he had ever floated the company publicly."

"Not greed then, but sex?"

"That doesn't follow at all. The more money there is in a thing, the more probable the greed motive."

"I suppose so," Kate admitted. "Bit disappointing, though. Sex is a much better seller."

Ignoring that, Henry went on, "Private companies

don't have to file detailed accounts at the companies' registry, the way public companies do. But they do have to list their shareholders. In that respect, Grossman Electronics is interesting."

"How?"

"Except for a few holdings by minor directors—qualifying shares, or not much more—there are only three principal shareholders. The nominal ordinary capital of the company is £1,000 in £1 stock units. You understand about nominal capital, Kate?"

"Not precisely."

"It's probably the capital with which the company was founded, years ago. And the nominal amount has never been increased. There must have been sufficient other security for the bank loans—the premises themselves, and perhaps other collateral put up by the directors personally, most of it by Grossman. He held 63 percent of the ordinary shares, and thus was absolute controller of the company. Presumably that controlling holding now passes to his estate, but we don't know who benefits under his will, or how much the control will be eroded by death duties."

"Obvious greed motive."

"Maybe. But put that aside for the moment. There remain the ordinary shares not held by Carl Grossman— 37 per cent of the total. Arthur John Coppock holds 15 per cent, and the minor directors two per cent between them. The remaining 20 per cent are owned by Mrs. Helga Rosa Grossman."

"Helga? Her name's Stella."

"I don't think it's his wife," said Henry. "The address given for her is Flat 1, 14 Gladstone Street, Loxham Bay. We'll have to ask Geoff about that."

"If it's not his wife, how come she's Mrs. Grossman? Oh, of course, his mother."

"Or possibly his sister-in-law, or the wife, or widow, of some more distant member of his family, a cousin perhaps."

"Such an advantage, a legal training," murmured Kate.

The telephone rang. She went to answer it. A couple of minutes later she was back on the balcony.

"That was Geoff, with news. There's been another hoax."

"Another?"

"The fire brigade called out to a farmhouse just outside the town."

"No fire?"

"No fire."

Henry stared at her, bewildered.

"But, Kate, that doesn't make sense."

The bar of the Royal Albert was already crammed with the men from Fleet Street. It was labelled at the entrance, in pokerwork on a hanging plaque of varnished rustic elm, the Oliver Twist bar; Henry groaned at the joke.

Why, he demanded of Kate, did the newspapermen on any crime story always settle on one bar in the town as the Press bar? So that they could keep a watchful eye on rivals, she told him, and pick up all the phoney rumours that were inevitably circulating among themselves. "Crime reporting's a form of incest, darling."

While Henry was pushing towards the bar to get drinks, she nodded and waved to her friends; she knew all of them, of course—the men from the dailies, several from the Sundays, including, she was happy to see, her old friend Dereck Andrews. She called to him and he waved back and started to push his way towards her.

At the far end of the bar a heated argument had started among a small group—photographers, of course, the most argumentative, loudly complaining men in the business. To her dismay she saw that the *Post* photographer was Horace, always the most truculent of the lot. If Horace couldn't manage to put the police backs up, he invariably grossly insulted the best contact Kate had made. He must have been the only photographer free, or Butch wouldn't have sent him. Butch knew how she felt about Horace. If there was anything nearer than the Congo River with a thicker skin than Horace, she had once complained to Butch, she had yet to meet it. Luckily Horace was now so vociferously engaged in whatever the photographers were arguing about that he had not seen her come in.

Dereck Andrews and Henry got to her simultaneously. Henry had spotted Dereck and bought him a pint.

"Thanks, old man. Have you been here long, Kate?"

"Since this morning."

"But the news flash didn't come through until mid-day."

Kate smiled happily at him. "By a fortunate chance . . ."

Dereck grinned. "Don't tell me. You were already here."

"Here or hereabouts."

"The luck of the Theobalds!"

"Sometimes you win," she murmured, "and sometimes you lose."

The *Sun* man struggled past her on his way to the bar. "Hallo, Kate. Bit late on the scene, aren't you? That's not like you."

"I expect I shall be able to pick something up, Joe," she told him demurely.

Dereck asked, "You know it's your old favourite, Roger Wake, in charge of the investigation?"

"I caught a glimpse of him—and he, I fancy, judging by the sour looks, of me. And I had a chatty exchange with Sam Kippis."

It was safe to tell Dereck anything. He was discreet, and her friend—and he didn't have to file a story for a Sunday newspaper until a couple of days later."

"Wake has called a Press conference for seven-thirty."

"Ah, that I didn't know. At the police station? Surprisingly co-operative of the aloof Mr. Wake."

"A few of the lads managed to get hold of the inspector, what's his name, Kippis—oh yes, you just said so. They put a little pressure on. You'll be going, I suppose. We ought to get moving soon."

"Come with us, Dereck," offered Henry. "My car's outside."

"Thanks. In that case," he said, turning for the bar, "we've time for one more drink."

For the conference they had to cram into the usual small office at the back of the police station, walls painted green, a few hard chairs, a scrubbed table, and everything with that institutional smell. Even with the light onshore breeze that had sprung up in the evening, the heat was stifling, sweaty. Kate was relieved that Wake and Kippis came in promptly; she couldn't stand this for long.

Wake was looking a little older, a little greyer, she thought, now that she had a good look at him. For all his antipathy to the Press, she knew no policeman she respected more—austere, silent, non-smoker, non-drinker, meticulously working by standard routine police methods and then illumining them with a vivid flash of intuition. Once he had introduced Sam Kippis, as he was now doing, as the police liaison with the Press, the reporters would see very little more of Detective Chief Superintendent Roger Wake.

The rubicund Kippis was talking now, in his best jollying voice. So far, there wasn't much to tell them. After a series of seemingly pointless hoaxes, which had all been false alarms, there had been a telephoned warning this morning that a bomb was placed in the Grossman Electronics factory. Contrary to natural expectation, this was no false alarm. An explosive device—he would not say a bomb—had been secreted in a drawer in the desk of Mr. Carl Grossman, the chairman of the company, who had been away on a business trip. When he returned and opened the drawer, the device exploded, wrecking the office and killing the man instantly. Experts were trying to reconstruct the triggering device, but very little of it was left.

Then the questions. Fingerprints? What sort of explosive? Was the drawer locked? Who had the keys? Any idea of motive? And so on and on—a babble. But

Kippis refused to say more. It was too early in the investigation. He would make himself available at the police station directly there were any more facts that could be released. The questions broke out again, but Kippis shook his head and followed the superintendent out of the room. The conference started to break up, disgruntled.

As she left, Kate's arm was touched by a constable. Would she please step through for a word with the super?

"I'll come with you," said Henry.

Wake and Kippis were in a small office off the station entrance hall. When she was seated, Wake gravely inclined his head in greeting. "I've read the statements that you and Mr. Hayward made immediately after the explosion, Mrs. Theobald. As you said to Mr. Kippis, they are rather brief and breathless."

"There was such confusion."

"Of course. It would be helpful if you would search your memory for every detail of what happened."

"I'd be glad to do anything I can to help."

"Perhaps we could talk about it in a few minutes," said Kippis. "Mr. Wake has to get away."

"Before I go," put in Roger Wake quietly, "I want to remind you that it's your duty to pass on to the police any information you may happen to come across that could be relevant to the investigation."

Kate smiled at him. "Not only to the police, Mr. Wake. To everyone who chooses to read the *Post*."

"That is precisely my point, and I shall leave Mr. Theobald, as a lawyer, to impress on you the seriousness of it. It is your responsibility not to publish anything that might impede the police investigation."

"That's something that your Chief Constable ought to discuss with my editor, Mr. Wake. My responsibility is to find out everything I can and report it to my newspaper. How much of it is published is up to the editor."

Wake gazed sombrely at her, silent. Then he said, "Mrs. Theobald, I know of old how enterprising you can be. I saw this morning that you were already prying into the somewhat delicate situation at Grossman's house."

"Delicate?"

"In the sense that Mrs. Grossman had just received the news of her husband's murder."

"Oh, I see," murmured Kate. But she was sure that was not what he had really meant. Something had almost slipped out; incredibly, for Wake.

"What I think you don't quite appreciate," he went on, "is the gravity of this crime."

"A murder."

"Most murderers in this country are not dangerous, except of course to the victim. They're domestic—husband, wife, lover, mistress. And most are committed on impulse by somebody who would certainly never commit murder again. But there's another kind of murder, now widespread, of which until lately we have seen very little in England—ruthless, violent, sometimes political as in the Irish or the Palestinian troubles, sometimes simply criminal, as quite often in the United States."

"And Carl Grossman's murder falls into one of those categories?"

"I don't know, Mrs. Theobald," said Wake cautiously. "Perhaps into neither. But the ruthlessness is apparent. I want to warn you, and your husband, of the danger into which you could run if you try to carry out amateur investigations on your own. This murderer is not somebody loosing off a shotgun, or strangling, in a fit of jealous rage. This is somebody deliberately using the methods of sophisticated terrorism, for reasons which, so far, we can only guess. The centres of terrorism are bound to throw out men who have become crazed with killing, perhaps simply for its own sake, but more probably for criminal gain. Mr. Theobald, as a sensible man impress on your wife how dangerous that sort of person could be to anybody who happened to get in his way."

CHAPTER 5

Nobody, declared Kate, could have called dinner at the Royal Albert anything but Brown Windsorish, slightly influenced by the Cypriot-Italian cults of escalope and pasta. Henry put it more curtly. They must find somewhere else to eat, or get a spirit stove and cook their own food in the bathroom. Though the claret wasn't bad, he admitted. Fairly mature, probably because they had so little sale for it.

But breakfast, in the same British hotel tradition, was excellent. They had it sent up and ate it in bed. Bacon, eggs and sausage, thick toast, Oxford marmalade and a huge pot of strong tea. While they ate, he passed her the newspapers. Front page in all, of course. "But nobody has the sort of show they've given me," Kate noted with satisfaction.

Henry put the tray out into the corridor and sat on the bed, his razor plugged into the nearest socket, while Kate took her bath.

When he had smoothed his chin, he joined her in the bathroom. "I've been thinking . . ."

"I shall have to stop eating that much breakfast," she mused, looking along her belly and thighs as she soaked in the bath. "I'm already putting it on round the hips again."

"Comfortable in bed," Henry said, "but perhaps a little too much when you're dressed."

"Oh, Henry, do you really think so? Damn. I must go back on a diet."

"That presents no problem in this hotel, if you cut breakfast."

"Pass me a towel," she commanded hastily, sitting up in the bath.

Henry began again. "I've been thinking. About those motives. We said sex or greed. But I believe Roger Wake was hinting last evening at a third—secrets."

"How do you mean, secrets?"

Helping her from the bath, and emptying it for his own, he said, "Something international. Defence, maybe. Remember what sort of factory it is, and the kind of man Grossman was. Electronics. He could have been experimenting on the quiet with new weapon techniques, say, in that factory. You told me that he was working on secret night-fighter devices during the war. He had probably kept up his contacts in that world. I wonder where he was on that business trip. Whitehall?"

"You read too many spy stories, darling. Pass me the talc. Be a dear and dab my back."

"No, seriously. Suppose he had the beginnings of something important, and he was discussing progress, as he went along, with Whitehall. There could have been a leak. That's where espionage starts, after all. If it were really important, there could have been people determined to smother it—by killing the brain devising it, maybe? It isn't impossible."

"All right. Third motive, secrets. So what?"

"You're the newspaper reporter."

"I'd say we need a lot more information."

"I'd agree with you."

"There's a redhead called Vera in the firm's office," said Kate. "She seemed to be everybody's confidante. Geoff knows her. She could be worth talking to."

The phone rang.

"You get it," said Henry, "I've got to bathe."

Kate wrapped the bath sheet round her and went to the phone.

"Geoff Hayward here. Am I calling too early?"

"No, no. I want to talk to you."

"I've made out a detailed account of the hoaxes. Damned if I can see any pattern."

"Shove it in an envelope and leave it at the hotel for Henry. What I want is to meet that redhead in the office."

"Vera Sanderson? That's easy. She lives quite near me. She'll be home today. Coppock has closed down the works for a couple of days until after the funeral. I'll pick you up and take you there."

"You come to the hotel," replied Kate hastily, "and we'll go by taxi."

From the bathroom Henry called, "Is that Geoff? Ask him about Mrs. Helga Grossman."

"Ah yes. Geoff, one of the shareholders in the company is a Mrs. Helga Grossman, living in the town somewhere. Know anything about her?"

"She's Carl Grossman's sister-in-law. She was married to his brother, who was killed in the war—in a concentration camp, I think. After the war, Grossman got her and her son out of Germany and gave her a share in his business to live on. The son's grown up now, of course, and gone off—he lives somewhere abroad, I think. Mrs. Grossman's a rather formidable old girl. Want me to go and see her?"

"Want Geoff to go and see her?" asked Kate.

"I'd rather go myself," called Henry.

"No," she told Geoff. "But you come round here as soon as you like."

She hung up.

"What do you expect from Mrs. Helga Grossman?" she asked Henry, giving him what Geoff had said.

"With luck, something about that company. She's the second largest shareholder. She must know something about it."

"You favour greed?"

"It's usually a much stronger emotion than sex."

Vera Sanderson lived in one of a colony of little bungalows in trim, suburban-style gardens that stretched up the hillside to the west of the town; just she and her widowed mother, Geoff told Kate in the taxi. They were comparative newcomers. They arrived, from London he thought, about three years ago. The mother did nothing except keep house. She wasn't seen much in the town; spent most of her time gardening. Vera had gone to work at Grossman Electronics as a typist, but had soon been promoted as Arthur Coppock's secretary. She did Grossman's letters too. "She's a smart girl."

The bungalow was near the clifftop and had a fine view over the bay. A couple of seagulls were planing overhead, crying hoarsely. Pleasant spot to live, thought Kate.

Geoff greeted a woman who rose from her knees, weeding a flower border. "Vera in, Mrs. Sanderson?"

"Yes, she's indoors."

"This is Kate Theobald, from the *Daily Post*. Mr. Coppock said she could have a talk with Vera about this dreadful business."

Mrs. Sanderson stood looking at them, trowel in hand. Not very communicative, thought Kate. She was a thin, pale, sunken-cheeked woman, looked ill. The reddish hair was greying.

Then the daughter came into the garden. Certainly a smart girl, and better-looking than Kate had noticed when she had first seen her in the office. An intelligent, lively face. Blue-green eyes. High cheekbones. Neat figure. And that really rather magnificent red hair.

"You remember Mr. Coppock said I could have a word with you," said Kate.

The girl nodded. "Come inside."

Kate turned to Geoff. "Why don't you take the taxi back to your car? I think one of us ought to keep in touch with the police, in case of developments. Send the taxi back here when he has dropped you."

The living-room of the bungalow had a wide window which brought in the view of the bay. The room was cheaply furnished, but in fair taste. Two of the pieces were good: a walnut corner-cupboard, a small knee-hole desk. There were several vases of well-arranged flowers, mostly roses from the garden.

Vera gestured Kate to a seat and sat opposite. "I don't think there's much I can tell you."

"It's chiefly about that telephone call. Whoever made it must have known there really was a bomb, and was probably the person who planted it in poor Mr. Grossman's desk. So it was most likely somebody who knew the offices and the factory well. Thinking back, do you have any recollection of the voice, any idea who it might have been?"

The girl shook her head. "I told Mr. Coppock, when you were with him, the voice was muffled. It was a man's voice. At least, I think it was. He said so little."

"Exactly what?"

" 'Warn everybody to get out. There's a bomb in the building.' Then hung up."

"Those exact words?"

"Yes."

"So then?"

"I tried to reach Arthur—Mr. Coppock. He hadn't arrived yet. We were only just opening. The assembly-line women were still coming in. I didn't know what to do."

"Terrible responsibility," sympathized Kate.

"Actually not. Not at the time. I thought it was just another of the silly hoaxes that had been going on in the town."

"Of course. All the same, when somebody talks about a bomb in the place you're sitting . . ."

Vera laughed. For the first time she was relaxing. "Slightly unsettling, yes. Then Mr. Coppock arrived and I simply told him."

"Were you kept long in suspense?"

"About ten minutes. He's usually punctual to the dot. But a phone call delayed him at home just as he was about to leave, and there was nobody else to take it."

"Mr. Coppock lives alone? He's not married?"

"No," said the girl. "He was, but it broke up—years ago, I think." Kate caught the look of embarrassment and smiled to herself. So that's where Vera's ambition lies! "He has a flat in the new block on the front."

"Nice flat?" asked Kate innocently.

"Oh yes, very nice." Then she slightly coloured.

Considerately, Kate switched the topic. "What's so puzzling is how the bomb was put into the desk drawer. I take it that Mr. Grossman always kept his desk locked when he was away."

"Always."

"Were there any spare keys?"

"Not at the office, anyway. I don't know if he had any at home."

"The bomb must have been placed while he was on his business trip. How long was he away?"

"He went to London on Friday afternoon. His business appointments were all in London on Monday and Tuesday. He wasn't supposed to come back until today. But he was recalled yesterday because of the bomb scare, so he only got his Monday appointments in. I had to cancel yesterday's by phone."

"So he was away from Friday afternoon until Tuesday morning. Why did he go for the weekend, if his appointments didn't start until Monday?"

"There was a concert at the Festival Hall on the Friday evening he specially wanted to hear. So he and Philip went up on Friday. I rang Smith's Hotel and told them. Mr. Grossman kept a small flat in the hotel permanently, mostly for business visits, and always stayed there. It's quiet."

"He and Philip?" asked Kate. "You mean Philip Sutton?"

"Yes. Have you met him?"

"He was breaking the news to Mrs. Grossman."

"Oh yes. Philip is Mr. Grossman's personal assistant. I do the letters, but Philip handles all the confidential stuff. He wasn't much good at it. I often had to help."

"Then why . . . ?"

"The music. Mr. Grossman is mad about music—or rather, he was." She suddenly started to weep. "That awful explosion! I can't properly take it in. I can't believe he's dead, that he was killed. What for? He was a good man. I ran up to the office when I heard the explosion. He looked . . ."

"I know. I ran there too."

The girl put her hands to her face. "I can't sleep, remembering it."

Kate sat in silence while Vera gradually regained control. At last she wiped her eyes with her handkerchief and looked at Kate again. "Sorry."

"My dear, I'm still shocked myself when I remember it—and I didn't know him."

The girl was steady again now. "Philip was trained as a violinist," she said. "He played in Mr. Grossman's quartet, at the house, twice every week. He was easily the best instrumentalist of the four, and I think that's what influenced Mr. Grossman to make him his PA. I'm sure he took him to London last Friday because of the concert. He wouldn't have needed him for the business appointments, and I had put up all the business papers he carried with him."

"Important business?" asked Kate casually.

"Not particularly. He went to London twice a month, and these were the usual calls—his lawyer, his patent agent, a couple of wholesalers for materials the factory uses, and three different meetings at the Ministry."

"Of Defence?"

"Yes. We do a lot of work for the Air Force, and some for the Navy."

"Secret work?"

"Well, I suppose all defence equipment is in some sort of secret category." She smiled. "We weren't making a death ray, or anything like that. At least, I don't think we were. Switchgear, mostly, and electronic rangefinders and such."

Kate considered. "So what it comes to is that the bomb could have been put in Mr. Grossman's desk at any time from Friday afternoon until early Tuesday morning—by anybody who had a key to the drawer. It could have been done over the weekend when the works are closed."

"I suppose it could," Vera agreed.

"Is somebody there all the time?"

"There's a security guard. We've a staff of four. There's always one on duty when the gates are shut. They work a roster for nights and over the weekend."

"So there's a record of which man would have been on duty, alone in the building, between Friday night and Tuesday morning."

"Yes. But they all would have been, at various times. No, I'm wrong. One's on annual leave. The three others would have been. But I assure you none of them wanted to kill Mr. Grossman. I know them all very well. They've been with the firm for years, and they're as loyal as it's possible to be. One's an ex-policeman, the two others ex-soldiers."

The phone rang. Vera got up to answer it, picking it up from a small table in the corner.

"It's Geoff Hayward, for you, Mrs. Theobald," she said.

Geoff sounded tense. "I think you ought to get down here as soon as you can. I can't tell you over the phone. I'll be in the snug, with our friend from yesterday."

"I'm on my way," said Kate.

She left without showing signs of haste. To Vera Sanderson she simply said that Geoff had received a message from her office in London, to call them. Vera invited her to make the call from that phone, but Kate said she'd better get back to the Royal Albert where all her notes were.

On her way through the garden she said goodbye pleasantly to Mrs. Sanderson, who straightened from the flower bed and nodded in acknowledgment.

"Back to the town," she told the taxi driver. "But I haven't got anything much to do before lunch, so I'll have a look around. Drop me off at the little fishing harbour."

The previous day she had noted the way from there to the Fishermen's Rest. It was less than five minutes' walk.

Geoff and Sergeant Bob Pace were seated on a settle at the back of the snug, pint tankards in hand, well away from the bar, where a young fellow stood chatting to the barman.

"I'll get you a drink," offered Geoff casually. "Lager again?"

"Please," said Kate, sitting by the sergeant.

Geoff came back with her drink and took the chair at the table in front of the settle.

"Well?" asked Kate.

Keeping his voice low, Geoff said, "They've caught the hoaxer."

"He's being questioned in the station now," said Sergeant Pace.

CHAPTER 6

When Geoff Hayward called that morning to pick Kate up at the hotel, he had handed to Henry his analysis of the five hoaxes in the town prior to the bomb at Grossman Electronics. Left to himself, Henry settled on the Pickwick Suite balcony to study it. There must, he told himself again, be a pattern.

The first hoax had taken place nearly a month earlier. Somebody had dialled a 999 emergency call and asked for "Fire." The phone operator switched him through to the town's fire station. The caller cried that a house was on fire in a terrace at the north end of the town; come quickly, or the whole terrace will catch. The fire engines raced out, of course. Halfway through the town the fire chief, travelling on the first tender, was puzzled not to be able to see smoke. But he had to go on, naturally. When the engines drew up, people emerged from several houses in the terrace to ask what was the matter. The fire chief knocked on the door of the house that was supposed to be ablaze. Somebody inside was playing the piano. The music stopped abruptly and an elderly man answered the door. Fire? No fire here.

The old man, Geoff had noted, is a music teacher, and he had been giving a child a music lesson in the house when the firemen arrived. "His name is Oscar Jenkins, a harmless old chap. But there's a connection with Grossman which I hadn't thought about before. Oscar Jenkins is the fourth in Grossman's quartet—the 'cellist. He's about the only 'cello player in the town. Carl Grossman grabbed him for the quartet years ago and, as usual, offered him a job in the firm, to free him for music, just as he later gave a job to Philip Sutton for the same reason. But old Oscar Jenkins didn't feel up to it. He preferred to continue as a music teacher, although he can scarcely make a living at it, I should think. But a year or two later he did ask Carl Grossman to give his son Terry a job in the factory, which Grossman did; something in the packing department, I think. Philip Sutton, by the way, was once old Jenkins's pupil—his star pupil, the only real success the old chap ever had. He taught Philip for years, until he got a scholarship to some music academy in London. Philip was away at the academy for three years, and then studied for a short while in Paris. Old Jenkins expected great things of him, said he'd be a concert performer, or get a place in one of the big orchestras. But Philip never did. He came back home, hung around for a bit not doing much, and then Grossman recruited him into the quartet, to replace a girl violinist who was marrying and leaving the town. And he gave him that job in the firm's office."

Geoff Hayward must be even thicker than Henry had at first thought, he mused, if he didn't see that as the start of a pattern. Grossman, and the firm, involved in some sort of indirect fashion with the first hoax. All Geoff had added was that too much time had elapsed for the police to trace the origin of the 999 phone call, but they thought it had come from a public callbox. The exchange operator said that he thought the caller was male, but he couldn't be certain.

Henry turned the page and began on Geoff's account of the second hoax. It was almost a week after the first. Late at night there was another 999 call, this time for "Ambulance." It was put through to the casualty ward at the hospital, and at the same time linked, on instruction, with the police station. The caller—definitely male—reported breathlessly that there was a terrible car smash at the White Lady crossroads outside the town. He had been passing in his own car a minute or so later, had actually heard the crash, and there were several injured people trapped in the cars, which were locked together. So he had rushed to the nearest callbox to get help.

The constable on duty at the police station, a bright lad, remembered that there was no callbox near the White Lady crossroads, and snapped through a separate line to the phone exchange to trace the call while the man was still speaking. It came from a callbox in the middle of the town. The constable came on the line to ask the caller for his name and address, but the man hung up. The constable was too late to stop the ambulance rushing out with the hospital's casualty doctor; the crossroads were, of course, silent and deserted. But he had a radio call made to the police car nearest to the callbox in town. That was also too late; nobody there or within sight.

Henry read the account over again, trying to find some link with Grossman or Grossman Electronics. But he could discern none. Perhaps he would be able to find one if he knew the local geography. He made a note to question Geoff Hayward on that point.

Nor could Henry find any link in the third hoax. This time it was an ordinary phone call to the Palace movie theatre. The caller said there was a bomb in the theatre, timed to go off fifteen minutes later. The manager, who happened to take the call himself, told the woman in the paydesk to ring the police and get them there fast. Then he got the projection box on the house phone and told the operator to stop the run and bring up the house lights. That done, the manager stepped out in front of the screen and asked the audience to leave quickly but calmly, since "an emergency" had arisen. All would have been well if a couple of young louts and their girls had not panicked and tried to push through an exit, knocking down the old woman who was trampled. Two older men had the sense to let the idiots out before they linked arms across the exit door and checked a panic. The old woman was detained in hospital for a week, but was not seriously injured.

No trace of Grossman in that. So what happened to the pattern?

Yet it recurred strongly in the fourth hoax. The call that time was to Grossman Electronics itself, the caller asking for Mr. Coppock. The switchboard asked who was calling, but the reply was that Mr. Coppock wouldn't know him, but it was a matter of life and death. Arthur Coppock took the call, feeling pretty sure it was a hoax, but having to listen all the same just in case it wasn't. The caller said he was warning that tubes of a poisonous skin irritant had been squeezed into the plastic containers of chemical paste used by women on part of the production line. Geoff could not remember the names of either the poison or the paste, but it seems they were chemically correct. A small amount of the poison named was in fact kept in one of the laboratories for use in a particular research project, and the containers of paste were easily got at, since no particular precaution would normally be taken about them. So Coppock had to stop the production line and remove the paste containers to the laboratory. None of the tubes of irritant poison was missing. But Carl Grossman insisted on himself analysing samples from all the paste containers before they were taken back to the line, to ensure that it really was a hoax, and they were uncontaminated.

The fifth hoax might have a link with Grossman Electronics, but there was no certainty about that. Again it was a callbox phone call, this time to the station manager at the town's railway station. A male voice said that a man had been seen to enter the north end of the tunnel under Grove Hill. The station manager took it for a hoax, but he was forced nonetheless to stop all trains and have the current switched off from that section of the line. A couple of experienced track-maintenance men were despatched to the tunnel. It took them more than an hour to search it thoroughly by the light of torches, for in that darkness an intruder might have hidden in a safety recess, then dodged past them to another. But at last they were satisfied that the tunnel was clear, and after more inevitable communication delays, the trains began to run again. The electricity cut-off had also stopped the industrial estate, and Grossman Electronics was the biggest outfit there; but not, of course, the only factory affected.

Then came the call which warned of the bomb that killed Carl Grossman.

Henry considered. Of the five hoaxes, two were clearly linked to Grossman or his firm, and a third, the railway-tunnel scare, did affect it, although that might have been by chance. Then came the sixth alarm, the real bomb. Three links, and a possible fourth, from a series of six alarms, certainly made a pattern in Henry's book.

But, try as he would, he could not fit the two other alarms into it anywhere. Nor could he perceive any time pattern in the intervals between the six calls; they varied, but not to any logical scheme.

The only factor common to all the alarms was that they had been given by phone, from callboxes; and, fairly certainly, by a male. Most of the people who took the calls said, on first questioning, that it was a man's voice. But then one or two wavered, not quite sure. Voices can sound odd in a telephone. Some women have deep voices, easily mistaken for a male. It is not difficult to disguise one's voice when talking into a phone. Vera Sanderson, who took the call about the bomb in the factory, was the only one to volunteer that the voice sounded muffled, as though in a deliberate attempt to disguise it. But when that possibility was put to the other recipients, two of them—the station manager and the duty fireman—agreed that it might have been so. The theatre manager would not commit himself. He had been too alarmed by the message to pay much attention to the voice.

Henry put Geoff Hayward's sheets of analysis into the desk drawer in the Pickwick sitting-room. He had been right. There was at least a partial pattern in the earlier hoaxes. It pointed towards Grossman's associates and factory, and culminated in Grossman's death. What the pattern implied was not yet apparent. Moreover, there had been one more hoax, a false fire alarm, several hours after Grossman was killed.

Henry found that perhaps the most puzzling fact of all.

If the series of hoaxes had a purpose—as he felt sure it had—what was the point in continuing it after the purpose had been achieved?

There was another curious thing that now occurred to him. The last call, the false fire alarm, was the only hoax that had been repeated. The bomb in Grossman's office was a repetition too—but that was not a hoax.

As he had remarked to Kate, that fire alarm, hours after Grossman's murder, simply didn't make sense.

Gladstone Street was a row of tall Victorian houses, not far from the centre of the town, overlooking a small grass triangle planted with half a dozen elderly trees. Number 14, like most of the other houses, had been converted into flats. There were two doors now in the porch that had once been closed by a massive house door. That on the right was labelled "Mrs. Helga Grossman."

Henry had to wait a long time before she answered it; so long that he thought she must be out, and he was turning to leave when the door slowly opened. The woman who stood there, leaning on a stick, was grey-haired, tall, stout. Her knuckles, he noticed, were swollen with arthritis. She wore a long dress of dark material almost to the ground, and a thin woollen shawl across her shoulders. But the impression of age was belied by her face—strong, angular, marked with traces of pain, and steady, watchful blue eyes. She was probably in her fifties, he thought. Thirty years earlier she would have been of striking appearance.

"Mrs. Grossman, my name is Henry Theobald. My wife is Kate Theobald, who writes for the *Daily Post*. You may have seen her account this morning of the dreadful murder of your brother-in-law."

The woman slowly nodded, but said nothing and did not otherwise move.

"I'm not a newspaperman myself. By profession I'm a barrister. But I'm trying to help her make some inquiries for her next report. She is most anxious not to get her facts wrong, and she has asked me to check on those she has about Mr. Grossman's career. He was, as we know, a most distinguished man, a brilliant scientist . . ."

The woman started to turn slowly. "You had better come in, Mr. Theobald."

Her voice was deep, with only a lingering trace of the accent of her German origin.

The room into which she led him, shuffling rather than actually limping, moving slowly with the help of her stick, was large and heavily furnished. Dark velvet curtains, massive chairs and settee, brown paintwork, an oak table with an embroidered runner, the walls hung with numerous framed photographic portraits in sepia, and big gilt-framed oil paintings of rural scenes, mostly forests or mountains.

Mrs. Grossman lowered herself on to a high-backed chair, like a throne, and motioned Henry to the settee. "What can I tell you?"

"You knew Mr. Grossman when he was young, I expect."

"Of course. He was born in Hamburg. His father was a doctor of medicine. His mother died in childbirth."

"He had a brilliant scholastic career?"

She assented. "First in Hamburg, then in Berlin. He was already a doctor of science at the age of twenty. And he was then engaged in research in a technical laboratory in Hamburg."

"Exactly why did he leave Germany in 1939?"

"It was not because he had Jewish blood, Mr. Theobald. There was a Jewish ancestor, but the Nazis were not insistent in the case of a scientist whose work was already appreciated by the Luftwaffe. Not only was he not compelled to leave Germany, he was not permitted."

"But he left."

"He escaped. There were certain undercover British organizations at that time helping to bring out men of Carl's calibre and outlook. He was helped across the frontier, and then brought privately to England, and lodged in a well-guarded house in the country, not far from here, which is why he started his own business here after the war. It was necessary in 1939 to protect such men as Carl. There were German agents trying to find them."

"And kill them?" asked Henry. "You don't think that his murder had anything to do with the events of those days?"

"No, no," replied the woman, slowly shaking her head. "It was all long ago, and is forgotten."

Henry got back to the mention of the business Grossman had started. She was the second largest shareholder in the company, and he wondered if she would let him have a look at the most recent balance sheets and annual reports.

"Why do you want that?"

He decided to be frank. "Mrs. Grossman, your brother-in-law was deliberately murdered. There must have been a strong reason. I wonder if it could have been concerned with the company. But very little information is published about private companies. If, possibly, something was going wrong—financial difficulties, disagreements, pressures from a bank . . ."

"There was nothing. Carl's business was secure and profitable."

"But there is still the possibility of disagreements—trouble of that kind."

"None that I know of. Carl and Arthur Coppock were the only two who mattered. They were always friends."

"You matter too, Mrs. Grossman. You have a larger share in the company than Mr. Coppock. You own one-fifth of it."

"Ah yes," she murmured, looking vague. "But I am not a business woman. Like Carl, I left all the affairs to Arthur. And now . . ."

She broke off. Henry waited expectantly, but she remained silent. Whatever it was she had been about to say, she had evidently decided not to.

After a few moments, therefore, he changed the approach. "My wife has met the present Mrs. Grossman—Mrs. Stella Grossman. But she would very much like a few background facts about Mr. Grossman's first wife. I believe her name was Phyllis."

"Yes," said the woman. Then, after a pause, she added, "She was not his wife."

"Oh, really? That is surprising."

Helga Grossman stared at Henry thoughtfully, in silence, for what seemed a very long time. At last she said, "You are a lawyer, Mr. Theobald?"

"Yes, a barrister, not a solicitor. I will gladly discuss with you any legal problem that is troubling you, but only privately and unofficially. If you want formal legal advice, you must go to your solicitor. I take it that you have a solicitor."

"The same as Carl. He is in London. Mr. Joseph."

"Of Scrutton and Joseph? Oh, I know him well. An excellent firm, Mrs. Grossman. You can rely on Mr. Joseph absolutely."

There was another long pause. Then she repeated, reflectively, "You are a lawyer, Mr. Theobald."

"Tell me what is worrying you."

"Anything I tell you, you must tell your wife, and she will write it in her newspaper."

"Not if it is something you tell me in confidence. My wife would never break a confidence. It's a newspaper tradition."

Helga Grossman considered. Then she said, "Well, I will tell you one thing. Carl was his parents' only child. His mother died when he was born—her first-born."

"But your husband . . . ? Oh, I see. Carl Grossman's father married again, and your husband was not Carl's brother, but his half-brother."

Slowly she shook her head. "I am not Carl's sister-in-law. I am his wife."

Henry stared at her. "You are his wife?"

"We were married in Hamburg in 1938. He was 22, I was 19. When he fled from Germany in 1939, I was to follow him after a few months. But it was too late. The war started."

"So that was why he did not marry Phyllis?"

"Oh," she said, "there was a ceremony."

"You mean, he didn't tell her?"

"He thought I must be dead. He thought he would never see me again. No, he did not tell her."

Now the story became obvious to Henry. After the war, the real wife reappeared with her son. So Carl Grossman was a bigamist. It would have been better in those postwar circumstances, Henry reflected, to have come clean. Grossman would have been charged, but probably there would have been no penalty. But, of course, Helga would have resumed her position as his wife, and Phyllis would have been out. Clearly, he had not wanted that. So he must have persuaded Helga to keep quiet. How? With the bribe of the shareholding in his company, of course. She got an income on which to live and bring up their child—by now it must have become a very considerable income—on condition that she posed as the widow of Carl's brother, supposedly killed in a concentration camp, but in fact never existent. It was neat enough. But was the woman telling the truth?

"Have you any documentary proof of your marriage, Mrs. Grossman?"

"You can read German?"

"Sufficiently."

She walked slowly to the massive oak escritoire, took a key from one of the small desk drawers and with it unlocked the bottom side drawer. She returned with a faded, shabby, brown-paper packet. Henry carefully undid the string and brought out the papers. His German was good enough for him to recognize the top document, a certificate of marriage, in Hamburg, on 12th March, 1938, between Karl Heinrich Grossman and Helga Rosa Schmidt. The records in Hamburg had almost certainly been lost in the bombing, but this paper would suffice. Henry had no doubt that it was genuine.

He looked up at her. "Why did you keep silent?"

"He had already gone through a marriage ceremony with Phyllis, before the war ended. He would have gone to prison."

"You did not mind giving him up?"

"I did not care, so long as I had security for myself and my son. I had suffered much during the war—too much to have any feelings."

"When Phyllis died you could have stepped into her place—a second marriage ceremony, maybe, to keep the secret."

She shrugged. "He did not want me, and by then I did not want him. I was comfortable. He had given me the shares in his business. I did not lack. A year later he said he wanted to marry another girl, a violinist, this Stella. I agreed. After so many years, why make trouble? For, if I had spoken, Carl would still have gone to prison, because of Phyllis. So I agreed. But now that he is dead, it cannot harm him for the truth to be told. And now that he is dead it should benefit me to be his wife. He was a rich man."

"You risk being accused of hiding the truth."

"I should say he forced me. Nobody would condemn me."

That, thought Henry, was probably true. "Did anyone else know of this, except Carl and yourself?"

"Only Arthur Coppock. He knew from the beginning. He arranged everything, all the business side. He has always known, but he has not said anything to anyone else, I am sure."

"Your son does not know?"

She shook her head. "There was no reason to tell him. Georg does not know. He thinks Carl was his uncle."

Henry handed back the papers. "Mrs. Grossman, get your solicitor here as soon as you can. Tell Mr. Joseph just what you have told me, and give him these papers. Then do as he advises."

Mrs. Grossman regarded him sombrely for a long moment, then said quietly, "I dare not get Mr. Joseph here."

"Dare not?"

"Yesterday I received a telephone call. A man's voice. He threatened me."

"What was the threat?"

"He was brief. He said that in a short while I would receive certain instructions. I must carry them out without question and without telling anybody. I must not make any move on my own without instructions. I must not go to the police. If I did not carry out these instructions, I would be dealt with in the same way as Carl."

"You have told the police?"

"No, I dare not."

"But it sounds like another hoax, Mrs. Grossman. You should ignore the threat and tell the police."

She slowly shook her head. "The call about the bomb at the works was not a hoax."

"Did you recognize the voice?"

The woman hesitated before shaking her head again.

"You seem doubtful," said Henry.

"At first it sounded like Arthur. But that is absurd. I think it was somebody trying to imitate Arthur's voice— but I have no idea who."

"Go to the police, Mrs. Grossman. If the threat is genuine, they will protect you."

"I dare not."

"Then why are you telling me?" asked Henry.

"I want you to take these papers to London and give them to Mr. Joseph. If he came here, the man who is threatening me might know. But the papers must be put in safety. I fear they may be taken from me."

"What you are really saying," Henry pointed out, "is that you do suspect that the man threatening you is Mr. Coppock. You said that he is the only man, other than Carl himself, who knew the marriage secret."

Mrs. Grossman moved uneasily. "No, it is not Arthur. There are reasons. Somebody else must have learned the secret."

"What reasons?" asked Henry quietly. Then, when she did not reply, he added, "If you want me to do this for you, you must be frank with me. I am not going to get mixed up in anything that I don't know about."

"Before he went to London last week, Carl came to see me. He said he was going to visit Mr. Joseph to alter his will. He would make various legacies which did not concern me, but there was one change I must know about. He was no longer going to leave his shares in the company to Stella. He was going to form them into a trust for charity. Carl wanted me to will my shares into the trust too, after making an income for my son."

"And you agreed?"

"No, I did not agree. I could not, for certain reasons. Seeing the question in Henry's look, she added, "Private reasons. Carl was angry, but that could not be helped."

Henry picked up the packet of documents which she had put on the table.

"If I take these to Mr. Joseph, will you promise to do whatever he advises?"

"But the threat . . ." she protested uneasily.

"Mr. Joseph will take that into account. What I think he will do is go to the police himself, and give them the information in confidence, on the understanding that they do not approach you. Nobody could then realize that the police had been told. Do you promise, Mrs. Grossman?"

After a long pause, she agreed. "Very well. I promise."

CHAPTER 7

Glancing into the Oliver Twist bar when he got back to the Royal Albert, Henry saw it was jammed with newspapermen, so he went up to the Pickwick Suite and poured himself a gin.

The phone rang. "Henry," said Kate, "there's been a development. I think it's phoney, but I have to stay with it for a while. Get yourself a snack, and let's meet at the hotel about three, to swap information."

It was half past three before she got there, joining him in the sunshine on the balcony, dropping gratefully on to a chair. "Phew, it's hot! Well up in the seventies. It was a phoney. The police thought they'd got the hoaxer. A cop in plain clothes happened to notice a teenage boy in a callbox, and his girl standing outside, giggling. He grabbed the boy and checked on the call he was making. It was to the police, reporting a swimmer in difficulties out at sea. A hoax, of course. The boy tried to bluff, but gave in directly they got him into the station. The girl had run off, but they soon picked her up. It's as Sergeant Pace said, that sort of thing is catching. The girl was terrified when they brought her in, and admitted she had dared the boy to make that false fire call yesterday evening."

"That's a relief," said Henry.

"Why?"

"It didn't fit. I'll explain in a minute. What have they done with the kids?"

"Kept them inside for a while, and they'll be charged in the juvenile court in the morning. They'll have to plead guilty, being caught actually staging another hoax. But they swear they weren't responsible for any of the hoaxes before last night. The police seem to believe them."

"So do I," said Henry. "That way, it makes sense. All they'll get is probation."

"I've phoned through a piece to the *Post*, to show how the atmosphere is working up," Kate told him. "With luck, I'll have it to myself. The police aren't likely to say anything until the kids come up in court in the morning. Geoff's friend Sergeant Pace is an invaluable source."

"You're not bribing?" asked Henry nervously.

"I would, darling. But there's no need. All the worthy sergeant gets is a few pints of bitter beer. Now, why didn't the false fire alarm fit?"

Henry produced Geoff's analysis of the previous hoaxes and went through it with her. "There's a pattern pointing to Grossman in three of the five hoaxes, and then what seemed like the sixth hoax but was actually murder. I admit I can't yet fit in two of the five hoaxes, but when we get more facts they may become clearer. But one thing is for sure. We don't yet know why somebody was working up to murder by that devious method. But once he had committed it, there would be no point at all in going on with the hoaxes. The corollary is, of course, that the hoax perpetrated after the murder is not the work of the original hoaxer, but of a stupid teenager showing off to his girl."

"You're convinced," she asked, "that the series of hoaxes was deliberately planned as a prelude to killing Grossman?"

"I think it's the only possible conclusion. And I also think that, if we can find out why, we shall know who."

"But so far?"

"Not a hint of an idea. Now, let's swap information." Kate gave him the gist of her interview with Vera Sanderson. "What do you make of that?"

"The first thing to note," answered Henry slowly, "though it doesn't seem to have any relevance, is that the red-headed Vera is in love with the managing director,

Arthur Coppock, and, judging by that slip about his flat, is probably bedding down with him."

"Noted," agreed Kate.

"Next there's the time factor. That needs thinking about. And, Kate, it narrows down very closely. Consider. Some time on Friday afternoon, probably soon after lunch—we ought to try to check that—Grossman locks his desk and goes off to London with Philip Sutton, his personal assistant. The works close down, I suppose, at 5:30. The security guards take over, and will have a note of anyone who entered the building between Friday evening and Monday morning, and then on Monday night. It's unlikely that the man with the bomb went in during those times. Too risky. The guards would know. But the bomb could have been planted, by anybody who had duplicates of the desk keys, at any time on the Friday afternoon. There would be no risk of a premature explosion. The desk drawer had to be unlocked and opened to trigger it off, and there were no duplicate keys at the office, Vera Sanderson says. So the bomb wouldn't go off until Grossman returned and unlocked his desk."

"You've limited the time too much," Kate argued. "Although the factory workers would have gone home at 5:30 on Friday, it's quite probable that some of the office staff would have stayed on a while, clearing up the week's work. So might some of the works people at foreman level. Then at some time, probably on Monday morning, or perhaps during the weekend, there must have been cleaners in the place."

"The duty guards ought to have records of all that."

"I doubt it. It was only a factory, not a defence establishment. And if they have to rely on their memories of who was there during all the closed periods from Friday evening until Tuesday morning opening, seems to me there might have been so many that a few could easily be forgotten."

Henry had to agree that it wasn't watertight. So they might be forced back on to the availability of duplicate keys to the desk, which would be much more difficult.

"Forget that for a moment," he said. "There are two other interesting matters in your interview with Vera Sanderson. The first is that Grossman's business did involve Whitehall. It slightly strengthens my 'secrets' motive."

"Vera said she herself made the appointments and put up the business papers he would need—and there was nothing unusual in their defence work."

"Doesn't mean a thing. If it were really secret, Grossman wouldn't have brought the girl into it. He'd have kept the papers locked in his desk. Damn! We've come full circle to those duplicate keys again."

They stared at each other for a few moments. Then Kate said, "Give it up. What's the other thing?"

"Philip Sutton. Grossman took him to London. You've seen him. What does he look like?"

"Quite handsome," said Kate, "and fashionably ill-dressed. Long hair, of course. Long thin face, a bit arrogant perhaps."

"Did he strike you as a possible queer? Or rather, what's the current word, gay?"

"You mean he and Carl Grossman . . . ?"

"The gossip that Geoff picked up might have got it wrong. Philip Sutton having an affair, not with Stella Grossman, but with Carl."

"I suppose anything's possible these days," Kate mused, "but it does seem unlikely. I think Sutton could be homo. But Grossman would have to be one too. And he has had two wives, the second one a humdinger. He seems very hetero to me."

"Or bisexual? After all, he took Philip to London, not Stella. They stayed together in Grossman's hotel suite."

"He is his PA."

"Not much good at it, according to Vera Sanderson. He has a sinecure because of his music."

"But that's it," protested Kate. "Grossman took him to London for the concert on Friday evening."

"Stella's a musician too. It's supposed to be their great common interest, isn't it? He didn't take her. And he spent the weekend in London with Philip instead of coming home. Loxham Bay's not all that far from London."

"Even if it's so, what has it to do with the murder?"

"I don't know. But there are possibilities. A jealous wife, for instance. She might well have keys to the desk."

"I must have another go at Stella," murmured Kate.

"And by the way," said Henry, "she's not his wife."

Kate stared. He told her of his interview with Helga Grossman. Kate's astonishment grew. "Rather trusting of her to let you have those documents."

"I think she was desperate. And, of course, I gave her my card and signed a receipt."

"Do you think the threat on the telephone was not just another hoax?"

Henry raised his hands in a gesture of helplessness. "How can one be sure? The police must be told, of course, and that's the real reason I agreed to take the documents to Bill Joseph. I can talk to him completely privately. It happens that we know each other quite well. We were at college together. I've phoned for an appointment with him tomorrow morning. It's the best way of informing the police, without putting Helga Grossman to any risk—if there is a risk, and not just a hoax."

"How much of this can I use, Henry?"

"Absolutely none, as yet. It was in confidence. Anyway, it's far too dangerous to touch. If there was a real threat, for heaven's sake don't get mixed up in it. When it does become public—as eventually it must, because in the end that marriage must be disclosed—I will work it so that you get what you call a beat."

"Henry dear, you're an angel. I shall tell Butch he owes you a session on scotch."

Henry smiled. "Don't tell him why. But say I'll lift a double off him this evening."

"You're going back tonight? You said your appointment with Joseph was for tomorrow."

"Yes, but early in the morning. I'll have to go up tonight. I'll go by train—you may need the car."

"Henry," she accused, "this is nothing but a plot to get dinner at your club."

He nodded calmly. "The alternative here is food poisoning or starvation."

At six o'clock Kate went down to the bar. With Henry gone, she felt like company. Every newspaperman was there already, naturally. Dereck Andrews saw her and came over. "Henry coming down?"

"No. He's had to go to London on business."

"Buy you a drink, then? Gin?"

"Lovely."

While Dereck was working towards the bar, Kate saw to her dismay that photographer Horace was approaching, accusatory.

"Look here, Kate, are we supposed to be on the same paper? That piece you had in this morning. You didn't tip me off."

"What was there to tip you off about, Horace? You weren't here when the bomb exploded. What else was there, pictorially, except a few of the people? I see you managed to get Stella Grossman. Nice work. And the managing director, Mr. Coppock, who was first on the scene. What else?"

"That's all very well," he said, slightly mollified, "but what next? What's developing?"

For a moment she considered putting him on to Helga Grossman, but quickly decided not to. She knew Horace. He would go round among the other photographers, looking superior, sneering, and soon letting them know he was on to something. Within half an hour they'd have got it out of him.

"Nothing that I know about, Horace," she told him. "Oh, there's Dereck Andrews coming back now. Be a dear and stick around to buy him a drink."

"Buy a drink for a bloody reporter?" Horace scorned, veering off.

She took the gin with gratitude.

"That was a great piece you had in the *Post* this morning," said Dereck.

"Mostly luck. I happened to be here, that's all."

"Your next story won't be luck. Anything I should follow up for Sunday?"

"Ask me on Saturday, Dereck darling."

He laughed. "So there is something. Okay."

The *Sun* man passed. "Apologies, Kate."

She smiled. "Accepted, Joe."

"I should have known," said Joe sadly, pushing on.

She felt a touch on her shoulder. "Hallo, Geoff. Dereck, this is Geoff Hayward, our man in this area. Dereck Andrews from the *Recorder*. Anything new, Geoff?"

"I'll get you a drink," said Dereck tactfully.

"Thanks. A pint."

When he had moved away, Geoff told her, "Bob Pace is very sorry he put you on to a stumer."

"But it wasn't. I think we've got it to ourselves until the kids come up in the juvenile court tomorrow. It made a nice background piece. Not sensational, I grant you. In fact, we're a bit thin for tomorrow morning."

"Well, there may be something. Bob Pace says we ought to go and talk to Oscar Jenkins."

"Oscar Jenkins?" she repeated. The name seemed vaguely familiar.

"The old music teacher. He plays the 'cello in the Grossman string quartet."

"Oh yes, I remember. The first fire alarm was at his house. Why should we see him?"

"Bob doesn't know. But the superintendent was there this afternoon."

"Good enough. Don't linger over your beer."

Geoff grinned and, when Dereck brought his pint, downed it in a single long draught. Dereck looked on admiringly.

"Rugger club training," explained Kate proudly. "That's the type of man we have working for the *Post*."

"Thanks, old man," said Geoff. "I'll have to buy you one next time."

"We've got to be off now," said Kate.

Dereck Andrews pleaded: "Kate, you know I can't get into print until Sunday. It's only Wednesday. You know you can trust me."

"All right," she agreed. "Come on. I've got Henry's car outside. But let's not make the exit too obvious. We really ought to find another bar. You go first, Geoff. We'll follow in a few minutes. Which will give Dereck just time," she added sweetly, "to buy me another gin."

The door was opened by Oscar Jenkins himself.

"Oh, it's you, Geoff."

He was a short tub of a man, peering through thin, steel-rimmed spectacles. A fluff of grey hair fringing a bald dome. Rather a dear, kind face, thought Kate, and a gentle though tremulous voice. An abject manner—or was it simply that, today, he was badly frightened?

"Here is Kate Theobald. You must have read her report in the *Post* this morning, Mr. Jenkins."

"That it should happen to Carl," the old man murmured plaintively. "I'm still not believing it."

"And this is Mr. Andrews, a reporter from the *Sunday Recorder*."

As though he had suddenly realized what was happening, the old man began to fluster. "Oh dear! Oh dear me, no! I don't think there's anything I could tell you for the newspapers."

"Hadn't we better go inside, Mr. Jenkins," suggested Geoff. "We don't want to attract attention."

For a few moments the old man hesitated, as though trying to gather enough courage for a refusal. But then he muttered something incoherent and let them in. Kate carefully closed the door behind them.

Oscar Jenkins led them to the back room, his music room. On the piano—upright and battered, but a Bechstein—were piled dozens of sheets and volumes of music, much of it simple tuition pieces. In one corner stood his 'cello, shrouded in cloth; a music-stand before it. A set of shelves on one wall held books, piles of sheet music, opera scores, a small white plaster bust of Beethoven, a packet of cigarettes and several boxes of matches, and an empty coffee mug. There were a few framed photographs on the walls, most of Oscar Jenkins in his best suit and floppy bow tie, surrounded by numerous children; no doubt music festivals at which he had adjudicated. His academic certificates, in thin black frames, hung among them. On the mantel shelf above the unlit gas fire were several more photographs, including a posed group of the string quartet, and a separate portrait of Philip Sutton, violin and bow in hand. On the wall above hung a large amateur oil painting of a formidable, middle-aged woman with a protuberant middle-aged bosom, in a bright pink dress. Kate wondered if this were Mrs. Jenkins. If so, she granted Oscar's manner to be abjection, not fright.

He stood in the middle of the room, looking uneasily around and making little plaintive noises in his throat, until they all found seats.

Kate began. "It's most kind of you to see us, Mr. Jenkins. Nothing to be alarmed about, of course. It's just that we're covering the dreadful murder of Mr. Grossman for our newspapers, and so naturally we like to have a word with anybody whom the police interview. I believe Mr. Roger Wake, the chief superintendent, came to see you this afternoon."

"Oh yes," admitted Jenkins, "he did. But I really don't think I should say anything."

Dereck Andrews held out a packet of cigarettes and the old man took one gratefully, groping behind him for a box of matches; but Dereck flicked his lighter.

"Oh, thank you. Thank you very much. But really, I can't say anything."

"Sometimes the Press can be helpful, Mr. Jenkins," put in Kate soothingly. "It's wonderful how misunderstandings get corrected when they're brought into the open. What did the superintendent want to ask you about?"

"Not me, but . . ."

Geoff Hayward connected. "Terry, Mr. Jenkins?" To

the others he explained, "Terry is Mr. Jenkins's son. He works at Grossman Electronics."

The old man suddenly straightened and stared wildly at them. "He had absolutely nothing to do with it. He couldn't have. It's absurd."

"I'm sure he had nothing to do with it," agreed Kate gently. "What happened, Mr. Jenkins?"

He turned to her, explaining, as though she was the one upon whom he could rely. "Terry was in the works at the weekend, that's all. Mr. Coppock asked him to go up on Saturday afternoon to fetch some papers from his office. Mr. Coppock had forgotten them, and he wanted to work on them over the weekend. Terry often ran errands for Mr. Coppock."

"Then the police simply have to check this with Mr. Coppock himself."

"Oh, they have, miss. And he confirms it, of course."

"Then there's nothing to worry about."

The old man hesitated, turned away, then looked back at her again. "It's the time he was there. He stayed for an hour or so. It's quite simple, really. Terry has an ambition to get into the production team at the works. At present he's only in packaging."

"So?"

"So he has been working on electrical circuits in one of the shops. The foreman knew about it. When he had got Mr. Coppock's papers on Saturday afternoon, he ought to have taken them straight to him, of course. But instead he was tempted, and he went to the workshop and spent an hour or more on his circuits. Of course, the man at the gate has the time."

"That doesn't sound to me very much to worry about either, Mr. Jenkins."

"He had absolutely nothing to do with the bomb," the old man suddenly burst out. "Why should he ever want to harm Mr. Grossman? Carl had been very kind to him, given him a job. Terry asked him for promotion to the production team, and I think Carl would have granted it in due course, even if for the moment..."

He broke off as they heard the front door open.

"That'll be Terry now," he almost whispered, the abject note returning to his voice. "They asked him to go down to the police station to make a statement. Purely a formality, of course. They explained that. His mother went with him . . ."

Directly Mrs. Jenkins came into the room, Kate understood the old man's abjection. She was the subject of the portrait over the mantel, and the artist had not exaggerated the aggressive protuberance of the bosom. It was matched by an equally protuberant behind. She was one of those women who carry themselves at a tilt, like a sailing-ship's figurehead.

"Everything all right now, dear?" asked her husband nervously.

Mrs. Jenkins gave him a quick glance of contempt, then demanded, "Who are these people?"

"It's me, Mrs. Jenkins. Geoff Hayward. Here is Kate Theobald of the *Post*. You'll have read her story this morning, I'm sure. And Mr. Andrews of the *Sunday Recorder*."

"And what do you want?"

Kate stepped in. There is only one way to deal with that sort of person. "The police have been questioning your son, Mrs. Jenkins. We're in touch with the police, of course. If you'd prefer us to get their account, instead of your son's, we will."

"What's it got to do with the newspapers?" Mrs. Jenkins asked, but now uncertain, defensive.

"A man has been murdered in a peculiarly horrible way. Your son is known to have spent an unauthorized hour or more on the premises during the time when the bomb must have been planted in the desk. I'm not suggesting for a moment that he had anything to do with it. But the fact that he was there will certainly be in the newspapers, very prominently. I should have thought he would welcome the chance to make quite clear what he was doing, and why he is beyond suspicion." Kate stared past the mother at the son, who had stood all this time just inside the door, his back to it. "Don't you, Terry?"

It was as though all of them had noticed for the first time that the boy was even there. He was about seventeen, Kate guessed; a pretty boy, with dark, curly hair, a round face, something of the arrogant bearing of his mother, but with timid, shifting brown eyes. He was slickly, immaculately dressed in an expensive, brightly-coloured shirt, a silk tie, beautifully-pressed fawn-coloured slacks, and brown-and-white leather shoes. The clothes must have been Mrs. Jenkins's choice. Boys of seventeen, left to themselves, do not dress like that.

As they all looked at him, waiting, he hesitated, almost pouted. "I don't mind telling you," he said. "It's the same as I told the police. I went to the works, Saturday afternoon, to fetch some papers Mr. Coppock wanted. While I was there, I spent about an hour on a circuit I'm working at, in one of the research shops. There wasn't any reason why I shouldn't. Mr. Coppock knows I'm doing it. He gave me permission. I'm getting some training, so I can move over to the production side. Mr. Coppock's promised me, when I'm good enough."

"Did you go into the office block?" asked Kate.

"Of course I did, to fetch the papers from Mr. Coppock's office. But I didn't go into Mr. Grossman's room."

Dereck Andrews spoke for the first time. "Did you see anybody else there?"

"Don't think so."

"Or hear anybody—footsteps, anything like that?"

The boy shrugged. "I can't remember."

"Why should he?" demanded his mother angrily. "Terry was simply fetching some papers for his boss. He had no reason to take notice of anybody else."

"Oh, quite so, Mrs. Jenkins," agreed Dereck soothingly. "I just wondered if he happened to see anybody, that's all."

"You're worse than the police, wondering, and questioning. You're not going to talk my boy into trouble, I tell you that. You'd all better go."

"I think perhaps we should," said Kate, getting up.

Turning to the old man, she added, "Thank you, Mr. Jenkins, for your help. And, Terry, don't be scared of talking. So long as you tell the police the truth, you'll be perfectly all right. It's when people try to hide things that suspicions start. Good evening, Mrs. Jenkins."

When they had driven away, Kate asked Dereck, "What did you think of that?"

"I think the kid was telling the truth, though with that gorgon of a mother . . ."

Kate laughed. "Formidable. And the poor little old music teacher, trembling in a corner, like a mouse."

"Anyway, the kid couldn't have put the bomb in Grossman's desk unless he had keys. How could he possibly have had them?"

"Somebody could have given them to him."

"Who?" asked Dereck sceptically.

"How do I know? But it's possible. The man who sent him to the factory that afternoon was Arthur Coppock."

"You mean, Coppock somehow persuaded the boy to kill Grossman?"

"I'm not saying so. But it's possible," repeated Kate. "After all, two men in a business association that is worth, according to Henry, at least a million—it's not difficult to suggest a motive."

Even as she said it, she recalled what Henry had told her of his interview with Helga Grossman. The name of Coppock was starting to emerge rather often, she thought.

Dereck was shaking his head vigorously, as though to clear it. "Now, let's talk sense. Even supposing, for the sake of argument, that the managing director had a motive for killing the chairman, he certainly wouldn't have brought in a teenage boy to do the job, or anybody else for that matter. Quite aside from the obvious risk of blackmail, a boy like that could be broken down by an experienced detective in a single interview. I doubt if it would take Roger Wake more than half an hour. If you ask me, young Terry Jenkins can't have had anything to do with it."

"He was there," Kate argued. "There is that curious gap of an hour or so inside the building. He had opportunity."

"But not motive. What possible motive could the lad have for wanting to kill Grossman?"

"A love affair?"

"Love affair? I don't follow. With whom?"

"With Grossman."

"Was he that way?"

"I don't think so. But Henry has his doubts."

"Good heavens, that hadn't occurred to me. I suppose the boy could be homosexual, with that possessive mother and downtrodden father. It's the classic pattern. But Grossman—I shouldn't have thought so. He was married twice."

"Possibly bisexual, Henry says. Or possibly cover girls."

"I still don't credit it," said Dereck. "But, even if it were so, and something had gone wrong emotionally, the rest doesn't follow. There might have been a fit of tantrums. But not deliberate, carefully-planned, sophisticated murder. He's a teenage boy, indulged and at the same time overruled by his awful mother. That could well make him a queer. But not a murderer."

"What it certainly makes him," Kate said, smiling, "is a damn good lead for my *Post* story tomorrow morning."

CHAPTER 8

Kate ducked Dereck's proposal that they should dine together. She had another idea vaguely forming. So she made the excuse of work, and left him in the Oliver Twist bar.

Geoff came upstairs and sat on the balcony while she wrote her new intro for the morning and phoned it to London. Then she joined him. The night was still. Beyond the coloured lights of the esplanade a moonpath shimmered gently across the water. Dance music could be faintly heard from the disco on the end of the pier.

"How well do you know Arthur Coppock?" she asked.

"Quite well. He's really my father's friend."

"Well enough to ring and ask if we may call on him?"

"Tonight?"

"Yes. Now, if possible."

"I can try," said Geoff, going inside to the phone.

A few minutes later he reappeared on the balcony. "I've got him on the line. He asks what you want to see him about."

"Tell him an interview with Terry Jenkins will be in the *Post* tomorrow. But say I'm worried about some of the things that young Jenkins said, and I'd like to check them with him."

Geoff went in again to the phone, then re-emerged. "Okay, but he says you'll have to be brief."

"Mr. Coppock always seems to want people to be brief."

"He's got a dinner date."

"With the redhead?"

Geoff smiled. "I shouldn't wonder."

The block in which Coppock lived was only a couple of hundred yards along the esplanade, so they walked, threading their way among the holiday-makers strolling in the evening air. It was a small block, but smart—all glass and wall-cladding and balconies. They took the lift to the top floor, the fifth. Coppock's flat was in front, facing the sea.

"Nice of you, Mr. Coppock," said Kate.

He grunted and led the way into the living-room; charmingly furnished, gently lit, opening through wide, sliding glass doors on to a large balcony equipped with a table, chairs, long wickerwork couches with bright plastic cushions. The table was laid for two. There was a bottle of wine in the cooler.

Coppock, no longer sweating in thick tweeds, but bathed and cool and spruce in a dark blue lightweight suit, seemed a different man from the one she had met so dramatically at the works. He was untense, calm, reposed, apparently friendly. What would they drink? Slightly astonished, Kate thanked him for a gin and tonic; Geoff took a bottle of beer.

"Now then," asked Coppock, "what can I tell you?"

"It's about Terry Jenkins." Kate told him briefly the story that Terry had given her; the same, he said, as he had given to the police. And old Mr. Jenkins said the police had checked with Mr. Coppock, who confirmed that he had sent Terry there on Saturday afternoon on an errand.

"That's right," agreed Coppock. "I was costing a job rather urgently and I'd left some of the papers on my desk."

"Old Mr. Jenkins seems rather a dear," said Kate.

Coppock smiled. "More than can be said for old Mrs. Jenkins, eh?"

"A dragon!"

"She has made that boy a laughing stock. You saw

how she dresses him? Imagine how the other kids treat him."

"Seems a damn shame."

"It's partly the reason why Carl took pity on him and gave him a job. But I suppose the real reason was to help the old man, for his music. You know that Oscar Jenkins played the 'cello in Carl's quartet?"

Kate nodded. "And you've been kind to the boy too, I was told."

"I've done what I can to help him. Terry's not particularly bright, but he has some sort of flair for mechanical and electrical work. Anyway, that's what the foreman reports. He shows an aptitude, and he's dead keen. The trouble is, he hasn't got an engineering diploma. He's taking a course at the local Further Education College, but it'll be a couple of years before he completes it. Meanwhile, we're letting him get some practical experience now and then in the workshops."

"In a way," mused Kate, "that's what has got him into an awkward situation."

"Is he in one?"

"The police had him in for questioning for quite a while. The fact is that he *was* in the works on Saturday afternoon, that he *did* stay for more than an hour which he says he spent in the workshop—but he has nobody to confirm that. He *was* on the executive office floor, because you sent him to your office. And I think it's clear that any suspect has to be somebody who knows pretty accurately what happens in Grossman Electronics, and so probably has to be somebody who works there. Don't you agree?"

"There are all sorts of objections to it," replied Coppock. "I suppose the chief one is that whoever planted the bomb had to have duplicate keys to Carl's desk. So far as I know, there are none at the works. Maybe he had a spare set at Warnham Court. But it's difficult to see how, in any case, young Terry Jenkins could have got hold of them. I simply don't know what to think."

"I put the keys question to Vera Sanderson when I

went to see her at her home," Kate told him, "and she said much the same thing—no keys at the office. I also said I thought that the man who phoned about the bomb must be the man who planted it, and was probably somebody very familiar with the factory. She said she hadn't recognized the voice. And she made no comment at all as to whether it must be somebody she knew."

Coppock smiled. "Then why not ask her again?" Raising his voice, he called, "Vera."

The redhead, wrapped in a flowered overall, appeared in the doorway to what must be the kitchen.

"I simply don't know what to think, either," she said.

"Twice a week," Coppock explained, "out of the goodness of her heart, Vera comes in to cook dinner for me. The rest of the week it's either a cut from the joint at the local Conservative Club, or *oeuf surprise* in the kitchen."

"Talking of eating in this gourmets' paradise," Kate took up, "where can one? The Royal Albert's so awful that it has driven my husband back to his club in London. I'm not a fussy feeder myself, but I must say I could do with something a bit more edible."

"There's a little Italian place at the back of the town which isn't too bad," said Coppock. He glanced, rather oddly Kate thought, at the girl.

She came in at once with, "Why don't you and Geoff take pot luck with us here?"

"How very kind," said Kate. Now she understood the glance. The invitation came really from Coppock. She wondered why. "But will it stretch?"

Vera Sanderson smiled. "All Arthur is getting on a night as hot as this is cold chicken and salad, followed by a can of peaches and cream. It'll stretch."

"Well, if you really mean it, we'd love to."

Suddenly stirring, Coppock exclaimed, "Past time for another drink!" He started to pour. "Are you sticking to beer, Geoff? There'll be wine."

"Beer and wine," quoted Geoff, "you feel fine. Wine

and beer, you feel queer. Not that I ever do," he added pleasantly.

"Such youth," sighed Kate, "such physique!"

"And let's drop the formalities," suggested Coppock as he handed her another gin. "Arthur and Vera and Geoff."

"Kate."

"Come on, Geoff," said Vera. "Lend a hand."

"Sure," he consented, following her into the kitchen, and emerging with the gear for two more places at the table on the balcony, then going back for the food.

When they settled to the table, Kate carefully kept the talk general—gossip, the theatre, anecdotes, the sorry state of politics, anything except Grossman and the murder. The meal was simple, but compared with the Royal Albert's menu, epicurean. The wine was delicious, a Pinot from Alsace, just sufficiently cooled to retain the flavour.

At last it was Arthur himself who brought in the Grossman topic. Geoff had cleared the dishes, Vera presided over a Cona of coffee, and they were all sipping Drambuie.

"It was good of you to steer clear of Topic A over dinner. But I assume you came here to ask me some questions."

"What I really came for," Kate admitted, "was to ask a favour. May I be shown round the Grossman Electronics works?"

"I suppose so," granted Arthur cautiously. "But why?"

"I've got to write about the place and I've no idea what it really looks like. All I saw was the entrance lobby and the office floor. I hate writing about a background I'm not sure of. It's so easy to make bad mistakes."

"It's just a series of workshops, like any other small-parts factory. But if it helps to see it, I suppose there's no reason why not. We're not reopening until noon tomorrow. The funeral's in the morning. I was going to shut for two whole days, but we're badly behind with a big export order, so the shop stewards agreed to make it a day and a half. Like most small factories, we have good labour relations."

"When is the funeral, by the way?"

"Ten o'clock tomorrow morning. The coroner has given consent to burial—in fact, cremation—without an autopsy. No need for that, of course. Scarcely practical anyhow. The actual funeral will be private, family and close associates only, at the village church near Warnham Court, and then at the town crematorium. Simultaneously there'll be a memorial service in St. Augustine's, in the centre of the town, to which the employees will go."

"The reporters won't," Kate promised him. "They'll be at the village church."

"There's nothing I can do about that," said Arthur wearily. "The Press must be served. When do you want to see the works?"

"When you reopen, if possible."

"All right. But Vera will have to show you round. I've been asked to keep myself available for a visit by Roger Wake. The police have searched the whole factory, and a special squad has been working in what remains of Carl's office, and now they've sealed that off. The superintendent sent a message saying it'll be necessary to question everyone who was on the premises that morning, but he would wait until we reopened, because of the funeral. Meanwhile he has added a couple of constables to each of the duty rosters of our own guards at the gate. They rang me to report that the police are making all the factory rounds with them, night and day."

"I won't be in the way," Kate assured him. "If I see Mr. Wake in the offing, I'll vanish. And thanks for letting me see the place. It really will be a help. By the way, since you said you were expecting questions, there is one vaguely troubling me. I find my thoughts wandering now and then round to young Terry Jenkins. He did have opportunity. What I keep wondering is whether he had any sort of motive."

Coppock looked incredulous. "For killing Carl? What possible motive could a young boy like Terry have?"

"The reporter who interviewed him with me, and met the parents, remarked afterwards that it looked like the classic pattern for making a boy homosexual. Is he?"

Arthur lifted the bottle and poured her another liqueur. "That's very perceptive. I don't know about Terry, in fact, but . . ."

"But the other side of the equation?" asked Kate softly. "That's not really my original idea. It was Henry's guess—Henry's my husband. He's a lawyer, and he thinks very straight. It's so useful for a newspaper person to be married to a lawyer. He thinks of all sorts of things that would never occur to me."

"Such as?"

"He got on to Mrs. Helga Grossman, just like that."

"How?" asked Arthur sharply.

"He asked our business editor for a rundown on your company. I should never have thought of that. You'll be glad to know you're highly thought of in the City. Though I suppose Carl Grossman's death must make some difference. I take it you'll keep the company running as usual."

"I've been running it for a quarter of a century," replied Arthur drily, "so I expect I shall. Carl never attempted to take part in the business side. He was the scientist, the inventive brain—and an invaluable contact with Whitehall."

"Can you replace him?"

"We don't have to, so far as the science and technology go. The head of the research laboratory can simply take over. Man named Fred Luxton. He has been with us for years. Carl brought him in from one of the university labs and trained him in our ways. Fred knows as much as Carl did about the stuff we're producing. Carl himself told me several times that Fred's the more brilliant scientist. But the gap will be the loss of Carl's personality, and his contacts. Carl was not only a scientist, but a man of the world—of the Whitehall world anyway. Fred's an academic. He lives in his laboratory like a rabbit in its hutch. He has virtually no outside friends or interests."

"No family?" asked Kate.

"A wife, no children. She was a science student too. Carl used to joke that they spent their evenings playing chess. But what you were going to tell me was how your husband got to know of Helga."

"Oh, that. The rundown on your firm included a list of the shareholders from the companies' registry. Carl Grossman had complete control, as you know. Who gets his share now?"

Arthur raised his hands expressively. "Stella, I suppose. But we shall have to wait for his will."

"Perhaps he left you control."

The man gestured again. "Who can say? All I know is that I'm the managing director—at present."

Kate thought it better to break off from that. "The second-largest shareholder was listed as Mrs. Helga Grossman. That's how Henry knew of her. So he went to see her. And she told him—but you know what she told him. You've known from the start. You probably don't want it mentioned in front of others."

Arthur Coppock looked at her steadily. A deliberate calm? she wondered.

"I can rely on Vera to keep a confidence, and I suppose you can rely on Geoff," he said. "Anyway, if what she told him is what I think, it'll be public soon. So what did Mrs. Helga Grossman tell him?"

"That she was Carl Grossman's wife and both the other marriages were bigamous."

She smiled to herself at Geoff's sudden whistle, and the girl's look of bewildered astonishment.

Arthur nodded. "Yes, I knew from the start. And now it's bound to come out—now that Carl's dead. Are you implying that it suggests a motive for his murder?"

"Not that I can see," said Kate.

"Have you sent this information to your newspaper?"

"Not yet. It's a confidence—for the time being."

She was about to explain about Henry going to London to talk to the Grossmans' solicitor, but stopped herself with sudden caution. She had had enough to drink, she told herself; keep your mouth shut, girl.

Fairly soon she made an excuse to leave. Her news desk would be putting through a routine call to the hotel at 11:30. So they rose from the table and Geoff helped Vera to carry out the last pieces of crockery, while Kate thanked Arthur Coppock for a lovely evening and rescue from the *table d'hôte* at the Royal Albert.

"Has your husband gone to London to follow up any inquiries suggested by Mrs. Helga Grossman?" asked Arthur casually.

"Oh no," she assured him. "Just vacation business of his own he has to clear up. I expect he'll be back tomorrow."

CHAPTER 9

She was right about the funeral. Well before ten o'clock the village church was thronged with reporters. An elderly verger tried to keep them out, but Dereck Andrews asked to speak to the rector, who was brought over from his house. He agreed to the reasonable request that the reporters should be allowed to fill the rear pews, reserving the half-dozen front rows for the mourners. ("It was because you had the forethought to put on a black tie, Dereck," Kate whispered to him.)

There was no question, however, of his allowing photographers to bring their cameras in. Any chance of persuading him was lost when Horace delivered an indignant harangue about churches having to stay open for prayers all the time, or they'd lose their licences, or whatever it was churches had to have. The rector's eyes hardened. He declared abruptly that there would be no photography in the church, and he required anybody with a camera to leave the churchyard immediately.

"I am now returning to the rectory to telephone the local constable to ensure that my wishes are respected."

The photographers complained bitterly that they had their jobs to do.

"You can take your pictures in the lane outside the churchyard," said the rector. "That is a public highway. I have no authority there."

He turned smartly and strode back to his rectory. Not much later a stout, red-faced constable arrived, parked his bicycle by the lych-gate, and unhurriedly moved all the photographers out of the churchyard.

The funeral itself was direct and simple, and the mourners few. Kate's only interest was in them. Stella Grossman was escorted, rather oddly Kate thought, by Philip Sutton. Arthur Coppock was accompanied by a tall, middle-aged man with a high bald dome fringed with dark hair. Four other men came in together. She assumed they were the minor directors and senior executives of the firm. She noticed Inspector Kippis, suitably black-tied, sitting unobtrusively to one side, almost hidden by a pillar. Just before the hearse arrived, a tall, stout, commanding woman had come slowly along the aisle, walking with difficulty, helping herself with an ebony cane in her right hand, and supported on her left by a stocky young man with somewhat similar hawkish features. Those two, Kate assumed, must be Helga Grossman and George, thought by everybody to be Carl Grossman's nephew, but in fact his son. He was, Kate guessed, in his early thirties. So Henry had probably been right to put Helga Grossman in her fifties. It was her lameness, and the dowdiness of her long dress, that gave the impression of age.

After the service was ended and the hearse and three following cars had driven away to the crematorium, Kate got hold of Horace. "Did you get a good one of the woman leaning on a stick, and the man with her?"

"I don't take bad ones."

"Oh, shut up, Horace. This matters. Did you get them?"

"Yes, of course. No thanks to you. If they're important why didn't you tip me off beforehand?"

"I didn't know about them, Horace, and I don't know now whether they're important or not. But when you send our stuff up, tell the office not to use anything of that couple, but to hang on to all the negs, in case they're needed later."

Horace fumed. "You're not going to tell me which of my pictures is to be used."

"Listen, Horace, are you going to send that message, or do I have to ring the editor?"

"But why?"

"Never mind why."

"Oh, all right," he sullenly agreed.

She would ring the editor anyhow, just in case, Kate privately decided.

By the time she had driven Geoff back to the industrial estate, the gates of Grossman Electronics were open and the workers going in. The police constable standing by the guard at the main entrance checked when Kate produced her union card. He had no authority to admit the Press. But the guard said it was all right, Mr. Coppock had telephoned to say she was coming, and Miss Sanderson was waiting for her inside, by appointment. Grudgingly, the constable let the two of them through.

Vera was already in the reception hall. "Now, what do you want to see? You can't go into Mr. Grossman's room, by the way. The police haven't yet unsealed it."

With a grimace, Kate said she certainly did not want to. All she wanted was a general look at the working parts of the factory. So Vera led them round.

It was as boring as are all factories. They walked first through the assembly shops where the line moved slowly along the brightly-lit benches at which the women sat, their fingers nimbly at work, their tongues gossiping to each other, their ears continuously assailed by sweet music from loud-speakers in the roof. Kate murmured that she could not understand how women stood it day after day.

"Best pay in the district," briefly answered the foreman to whom Vera had correctly handed over conduct of the inspection.

As they passed, most of the women ceased their chatter and watched them with curiosity. One or two made cheerful jokes about the Press, arousing giggles. But the nimbleness of the fingers continued unabated; and so did the rhythmic torture from the roof.

Beyond lay the pressing shops, where parts were stamped out of metal, or ingeniously and with remark-

able speed frabricated from molten plastic. Here the
workers were mostly men. And here the music seemed
quieter—but only because the machines were so much
noisier.

"Those are the two main sections," explained Vera.
"There are a few ancillary services, such as packaging
and dispatch. But the only other interesting parts of the
works are the design offices and the research labs."

"Packaging and dispatch is where young Terry Jenkins
works?"

"Yes. It's beyond the assembly lines, of course. It's
close to the labs."

The department itself was the usual array of packing
benches, forklift trucks, stacks of goods for packing at
one end, and large cartons of packed goods being loaded
into trucks backing in from the yard beyond. Kate looked
swiftly along the lines and spotted Terry driving one of
the forklifts. He quickly turned his eyes away from her
direction. Even driving a forklift, Kate noticed with
amusement, he contrived to look fancily dressed. In the
heat, most of the men were stripped to the waist. He had
retained a neatly-checked, opened-necked, short-sleeved
shirt, and his jeans were creased down the front.

"Where's the shop where he was working on that circuit?" asked Kate.

"I'm not sure. But it must be in the design and research block—through this door and along the corridor,"
Vera told her.

Here, mercifully, there was no music relay. In addi-
tion to the top lighting there were adjustable lights over
the drawing-boards and the construction benches. Half
a dozen men and three women were working in silence—
the silence of concentration.

Vera led the way into a small, glass-partitioned office
at one end. The occupier had just come in and was hanging his black jacket on a peg. As he turned, Kate recognized the tall, balding man who had been with Arthur
Coppock at the church.

Vera introduced him. "Dr. Luxton. As Arthur told

you last night, Dr. Luxton is now the firm's chief scientist."

"To my grief," he said. "I'd have wished anything sooner."

The moment he spoke, Kate liked him. There was still in his throat a trace of a northern accent; Liverpool, she guessed, but it might have been anywhere around Manchester. He gave the impression of a calm, unhurried, simple person. Not ambitious. The grief, Kate felt sure, was real.

"Are you better now, Dr. Luxton?" asked Vera.

"On the mend, thanks."

"This is Kate Theobald from the *Post*. Did Arthur warn you she was coming?"

"He spoke of it on the way to the church. Good morning, Mrs. Theobald. What can I tell you?"

"I really just want to have a general look around the factory, to get the background of what I'm writing about."

"She has seen all the workshops and the design office. There's only the research labs."

"Whether I should show you . . ." began Luxton doubtfully.

Kate assured him that she did not want to pry into any secrets.

"It's not that," he said. "There's nowt very secret about what we're doing at present, though it's defence, so naturally it's not talked of. It's booby-traps."

"You're making booby-traps?"

He laughed. "Nay, not making them. Experimenting with ways of coping with them. You know the toll they've taken of our lads in Northern Ireland. What Carl Grossman put up to the Army people was his idea that, by using our sort of electronic techniques, we could work out counter weapons. Do you know much about explosives, Mrs. Theobald?"

"Not a thing."

"Then I'll not be technical. The basic booby-trap is a bucket of water fixed up over a door left just ajar. Whoever opens the door gets the water all over him. Instead of the bucket of water, you've got explosive, with a detonator already armed—ready to be triggered off. Instead of the door that's ajar, you have something else that triggers the detonator. It can be as simple as a thin cord stretched across a dark passage that anyone who walks there will knock with his legs. It can be much more complicated—a beam focused on an electric cell, say, that triggers the device when somebody walks through the beam and cuts it off from the cell. The trigger can be set off from a distance—quite a long distance—by radio control. And there are much more sophisticated triggering devices that, luckily, most of the murdering brutes miscalled terrorists haven't yet got around to."

"So your line of approach?" asked Kate.

"We have two. The first is comparatively easy. It's a device for detonating any charge in a building from outside. Troops going to search a building can operate it before they go in and, if there's any kind of booby-trap there, it'll explode. Essentially, of course, it saves lives, which is the important thing. But it still wrecks the property. So Carl Grossman, who was a genius, Mrs. Theobald, had a second line of approach. The idea was still to operate from outside a building, not to explode the charge, but to disarm any known form of detonator."

"Had he got it?"

"This is secret information—not for your newspaper?"

"I promise."

Dr. Luxton looked at her for a long moment, then seemed to decide he could trust her. "Damn near. Not quite there, but close. Damn close. If he'd lived, I'd have said it was a certainty. Now it's left to me. Well, I shall do my best, and hope. Carl had solved most of the problems. Just a couple more, and the world'll be a safer place. But don't ask me any more."

"Not a thing. And it's absolutely off the record. Let's get back to the awful business of the murder. Have you any idea, Dr. Luxton, of what sort of bomb was put in Mr. Grossman's desk?"

He stared at her again. "I'm fairly sure I know. I told that police superintendent when he called at my house yesterday. I've been away sick for a week—a touch of summer 'flu. I'm not fully recovered yet, but of course I had to go to Carl's funeral."

"So the bomb . . . ?"

"Downstairs we've got a fortified cellar—a sort of blastproof bunker. Almost soundproof too, for the small explosions we are experimenting with. In order to try to find a way to neutralize booby-traps we first had to have the things themselves to work on, of course. The Defence Ministry sent us samples that had been found and de-fused before they could be operated. Other kinds, Carl and I made up for ourselves."

It took a moment for Kate to grasp what he was say-ing. Did he mean that Mr. Grossman was killed with one of the booby-traps from the research bunker?

Dr. Luxton nodded. "Almost certainly. But I can't prove it. Carl was working down there last Friday morn-ing. He telephoned me at home to talk about it—techni-cal talk. But I don't know how many of the devices he exploded. The only record of it was in his desk, where he always kept his research log. All papers in the desk were either destroyed or burned beyond deciphering."

Kate asked, "If it was one of the booby-traps from the bunker . . . It's kept locked, I suppose? Yes, of course. Who had access to the keys?"

"I have one. It never leaves the keychain I always wear. Carl had a key, but he didn't carry it with him. Spoilt the shape of his clothes, he used to say, poor devil. He had his vanities, like all geniuses. He kept his factory-key bunch locked in his office desk."

"And only he had access to it?"

"When he was away, yes. But when he was in the build-ing, I don't suppose his desk was locked all the time. Several people could have had access—that pansy PA of his for one."

"And Mr. Coppock?"

"He wouldn't need it. He had his own personal set of

all the factory keys. I don't know where he keeps them, but somewhere safe, you can be sure. Mr. Coppock is a methodical man."

"Are there other keys to the bunker?"

"The fireman or guard on watch has one, in the duty room. Has to have, in case a fire breaks out anywhere in the building. First priority for a couple of firemen is to get the explosives out and into the open. It wouldn't take long. There's not all that much in there. You don't need a lot for research experiments."

"Have the police checked on the duty-room key to the bunker?"

Dr. Luxton smiled. "You'd better ask the police."

"Fair enough," agreed Kate. "But tell me one thing more. Exactly what sort of booby-trap do you reckon was in Mr. Grossman's desk drawer?"

"Not in the drawer. When the police came to my house yesterday, the superintendent brought what was left of the device, to see if I could identify it."

"Could you?"

"It was a small limpet bomb, probably stuck somewhere under the knee-hole of the desk. It was a big desk, with plenty of room underneath. It was a simple type of booby-trap, not all that large, but sufficient to destroy the desk and kill anyone nearby. And it must have been triggered by a quite elementary device, directly the drawer was opened. There seems to have been a contact mat under the desk rug too, so that the thing wasn't activated until somebody was sitting in the chair. Anyone could sit there without opening the drawer and be safe. Or open the drawer without sitting down and be safe. The only person who would sit in the chair, and then unlock and open the drawer, would be Carl himself. Simple, but fiendish."

Suddenly Kate realized the implication. "You mean the person who set the trap didn't have to open the desk drawer to do so?"

"Of course he didn't. It was all on the outside. I told you, a limpet bomb. The only role played by the drawer

was to trigger the device fixed under the desk when somebody sitting in the chair unlocked and opened it."

"So whoever planted that bomb to kill Carl Grossman
did not need to have keys to his desk?"

"Of course not."

Which altered the whole thing, Kate saw. The keys to
the desk no longer had any significance. Anybody with
access to Grossman's office, at any time after he left for
London on the previous Friday afternoon, could have
set the trap in a few minutes, and been 99 per cent sure
that the only person it would kill could be Carl Grossman.

Dr. Luxton's gentle cough startled her. She apologized
for inattention. She was thinking.

He smiled, and advised her not to blame herself for
that. "Do you want to see the bunker?"

"Please."

He led the way down the stairs to a steel door at the
foot. Pulling keys on a long chain from his pocket, Dr.
Luxton unlocked the door. But before he opened it, he
turned with a caution.

"The drill is, always to enter the lab carefully. It con-
tains high explosive. When you get inside, you'll find low
blastwalls on each side of the central approach aisle.
Stay behind them until I tell you to come on. What you
will then see is a set of four blast-chambers, thickly protected, with a bench in each on which the various booby-
traps are set up. There's nothing to be alarmed about.
They are never left armed—ready to be fired, that is.
But I shall make a precautionary check, because nobody
has been in here—or should have been—since Carl left
the place and locked it behind him last Friday morning.
So I go through a checking drill." He smiled at Kate.
"Do you ski?"

"Yes, fairly well. Henry's a dab at it. Henry's my
husband."

"Then you may have seen, on the high slopes in Switz-
erland, a permanent notice—remember you are on a

mountain, don't take risks. I could say the same down this blast bunker. Don't take risks. Remember you're among high explosives."

He turned and opened the door, switching on a brilliant ceiling light. Dr. Luxton moved in.

Kate asked Vera, "Are you coming in?"

"No, thanks. I've seen it before. It scares me stiff."

"That's a great comfort," murmured Kate.

"Come on," said Geoff, taking her arm and propelling her into the room. He turned to the left, and they stood side by side, as instructed, behind the breast-high blast-wall.

Dr. Luxton was at a central switch panel, going through the routine check. Lights flickered one by one on the panels behind the benches in each of the blast-chambers. On the benches were fixed numerous small objects, boxes, canisters, a lot of complicated wiring.

Suddenly Luxton shouted, "Get down!"

Geoff jerked Kate to the floor just as there came the little crack of the explosion and her nostrils were filled with the acrid sensation of smoke.

CHAPTER 10

The appointment Henry had made with the Grossmans' solicitor, William Joseph, was for ten o'clock on that Thursday morning, at the offices of Messrs Scrutton and Joseph in Lincoln's Inn.

Bill Joseph welcomed him, remarking that they had scarcely met since their college days, and that Henry looked remarkably well, and was accumulating (so Bill Joseph was informed) a substantial law practice at the Bar; which last remark Henry modestly deprecated, while admitting that he was able now and then, by the mercy of heaven, to make a bob or two.

The preliminary courtesies over, Joseph turned with some curiosity to the reason for the appointment. "I gathered from my secretary, to whom you talked on the phone yesterday, that it has something to do with the Grossmans. I didn't know you knew the family."

"I don't," said Henry, "except by chance."

He explained that he was accompanying his wife while she reported the murder for her newspaper, and had gone to see Mrs. Helga Grossman to obtain some information. A formidable person!

"So I've heard," agreed Joseph. "I should tell you that the Grossman affairs were really my father's business, for many years. But he retired a year ago, and they were passed to me. Since then, Carl Grossman has called on me every time he came to London, which was at least once a month, often twice. I met his wife once, at a drinks party—lovely drop of woman, but a bit inscrutable, I thought. I've not met the sister-in-law at all."

Henry smiled. "You're just about to have to revise almost all those remarks, Bill."

"Revise? I don't understand."

"Mrs. Helga Grossman asked me to bring these documents to you, for safe keeping, and advice." He took a large envelope from his briefcase. "I've come to see you at her request. How's your German?"

"Schoolboy level."

"That'll do, to get the gist," said Henry, handing over the envelope.

Mystified, Joseph took out the documents and began to read. In a few moments he looked up at Henry, bewildered. "She seems to be claiming to be Carl's wife—or rather, widow."

Henry assented. "And subject to expert examination of the documents—which is probably all that's possible, because the original German records were almost certainly destroyed during the war—the claim seems to me to be good!"

"But why . . . ?"

"Why wait until now? When she turned up in England with their son after the war, Carl was already married to an Englishwoman, Phyllis—bigamously, of course. So he bribed Helga to keep quiet and pretend to be his widowed sister-in-law, by giving her a one-fifth share in the little electronics firm he had just started. When Phyllis died, Carl was still vulnerable, of course, and when he wanted his second so-called wife, Stella, the real wife agreed to continue to keep silent. She didn't want him herself by then. She told me this yesterday. All she wanted was the security of the income from the company —which must by now have grown into a very considerable income indeed."

"If only she could have kept it," murmured Joseph.

"Hasn't she?"

Joseph shook his head. "We're speaking absolutely privately and unofficially, I take it."

"Of course."

"Strictly irregular! But if we can talk on that basis, as

private friends, I'd very much value your views, Henry. Because it's a damn difficult situation—even more difficult than you know."

"We're talking as friends. What has happened to the old girl's money?"

"George—or, as she still calls him, I believe, Georg."

"Carl Grossman's son?"

Joseph stared at him in dismay. "Good grief! That's another complication. He isn't Carl's son. He can't be. Carl Grossman fled from Germany in 1939. Helga arrived here in, I think, 1946, with a child in arms. The question never arose before. George was supposed to be Carl's nephew. But now . . ."

"So she was living with another man in Germany."

"Perhaps. Who knows what happened in the European chaos when Germany collapsed? She was in Berlin when the Red Army got there and raped every woman in sight. Maybe George is half Slav. It wasn't an uncommon story."

Henry said, "Never mind about George's origins. What about his mother's money?"

Joseph paused, considered carefully, then told him, "This bit must be specially confidential. Young George is a bad hat. Some years ago, when he was in his early twenties, he came to live in London and got mixed up with criminals. My father, who knew a little about it, told me that it started with a woman he got hold of, a prostitute. It was before the worst London gangs were broken up, and George got involved with one of them. Father kept clear of the whole thing as much as he could. He simply didn't want to know. Carl Grossman consulted him once, he told me, about his nephew—as George was then assumed to be. Carl told my father he had no intention of rescuing the boy from any trouble he got into, and George was to be told so if he tried anything with the family solicitors. I believe he did once. He tried to raise a loan. Father sent him off with a flea in his ear. Father thought at that time that Carl was at fault in not helping his brother's son. But one sees now that Carl simply detested his real wife's bastard. Oh dear me, it is difficult."

"And Helga's money?"

"I don't know the details. A few years ago she came to my father and said she needed £10,000. Father advised her to go to Carl, but she said that wouldn't do. Father therefore assumed—correctly, I'm sure—that it was something to do with her son. She said she would have to sell her shares in Grossman Electronics. Father had to tell her that she couldn't, unless Carl approved, because there's a clause in the company's articles permitting the Board—in effect, at that time, Carl Grossman himself—to refuse to register a change of ownership of shares in the company. And he wouldn't have done so to help young George. You can see that, in those circumstances, it wouldn't have been any use passing her over to a bank. She couldn't pledge shares she hadn't an unrestricted right to sell."

"What happened?"

"Some short time later she wrote to my father, telling him that she had arranged the matter privately, and he need not concern himself with it any more. Later, he heard through other channels that Helga was damned hard up, and that Carl was refusing to help her."

"She could have blackmailed him into giving her the money," Henry pointed out.

"By threatening him with these documents? Yes, I suppose she could. But I'm sure she didn't. According to my father, she's an austere, essentially upright and honest woman. I don't know how she raised the £10,000. She probably found some way of pledging those shares."

"She's still on the register as owner of them," Henry told him. "I had it looked up."

"No doubt. She would have to be, because of the company's articles. But there must have been some loophole, some way of raising that money. She needed it to get George out of trouble. Her idea, I gathered from my father, was to get him away to Australia."

"Real trouble?" asked Henry. And when Joseph nod-ded, he added, "And is he still in Australia?"

Joseph looked embarrassed. "Don't press me on that, please Henry. I don't know where George is now—and, frankly, I don't want to know, now or ever." His gaze returned to the German documents on his desk. He grunted unhappily. "Every time I look at these I see a new complication. If they're genuine, Helga will be able to contest Carl's will. And that's a mess too."

Henry looked inquiringly but said nothing.

After a doubting pause, Joseph went on, "Carl came to see me on Monday, the day before he was killed. I told you he always came to see me when he was in Lon-don, as part of his business routine. But this wasn't routine. He tended to be a vindictive man, you know. There must have been some colossal row with his wife—I mean his supposed wife, Stella. Oh hell, let's stick to their first names. He wanted to see the will he had made just after he married her. Well, I had the file brought in. It contained a draft of that will, leaving most of what he owned to Stella, but there was no actual will. The only signed and witnessed will we had had was the one he had made years earlier, after he married Phyllis. Ac-cording to the notes in the file, it left the bulk of his estate, including his shares in Grossman Electronics, to Phyllis. I told him that, since he had subsequently mar-ried Stella, the Phyllis will was no longer valid. In fact, of course, since he wasn't legally married to Stella, that earlier will would have been good, and Phyllis's next-of-kin would be about to receive a very large legacy. But as it happened he had instructed, on his marriage to Stella, that the Phyllis will should be destroyed, and it was."

"What about the Stella will?"

"Carl insisted that he had signed it. So I phoned my father at home, while Carl was still in the office. Father confirmed that the will had been drawn up and sent to Carl, but had never been completed, so far as he knew. Certainly it had never been returned to us. Father had been on to Carl about it at the time, of course, and Carl had told him he was no longer to concern himself with the matter. Carl Grossman was often abrupt like that.

"When I put the phone down and told Carl what my father had said, he had the grace to apologize. Yes, that was correct. He had forgotten. But he had executed the Stella will, and he had it quite safely, down at Loxham. He had handed it for safe keeping with the firm's vital documents to his business colleague, Arthur Coppock, who looked after all his business affairs for him. When he got back, he would tell Coppock to send it to me. For he intended to change it. He then discussed the changes he wanted to make. I took notes, of course. Apart from a few minor legacies, he wanted all his property put into a trust for the benefit of charities. He would let me know in due course which charities. I made the usual noises about his wife Stella. He told me to mind my own business. Then I said it was my duty to point out how unsatisfactory it would be to vest control of a manufactory in a charitable trust. I advised it would be preferable to convert Grossman Electronics from a private to a public company, getting a quotation for the shares on the Stock Exchange. Then, on his death, his shareholding could be disposed of to settle estate duty, and as to the remainder for the benefit of the charitable trust; and the continuity of the firm itself would be safeguarded. He agreed with that, and told me to start making the necessary preparations for going public next year. But I was to let him have a draft of the new will straight away."

Henry said. "And there was no time."

"Obviously. I never got further than my notes. He was killed next morning."

"Has Coppock got into touch about the will?"

"Not a word. That's a bit odd."

"Perhaps," suggested Henry, "Carl didn't hand over the will to Coppock, but kept it among his own private papers. So Coppock would assume it was in your keeping."

"Perhaps. Carl was very absent-minded about business matters, which is why he usually left them to Coppock.

He had the other-worldliness of an inventive genius—
which he certainly was."

"Anyway," mused Henry, "Stella gets the jackpot.
Lucky Stella. Do the police know?"

"Not yet. I've had a letter from the Chief Constable of
the county, asking me to give any information required
by a Detective Chief Superintendent Roger Wake. And
Mr. Wake himself telephoned yesterday to ask if he
could come to see me. I think that, in view of these German documents, I'd better go down there to see him."

"I imagine," agreed Henry, "that his interest will be
both professional and acute. Stella the beneficiary. Well,
well!"

"But is she?" interposed Joseph. "According to our
copy of the draft—which, of course, he may have altered
before he signed—she is named as "my wife." Since she
isn't his wife, and it's a bigamous union, does that invali-
date the bequest?"

Henry laughed. "What you need on that point is counsel's opinion. And what counsel needs is a private half-
hour with his books."

"I'll have to get down there promptly," Joseph considered. "I'd better go this afternoon. Have you got your
car here, or can I give you a lift?"

"Thanks, but I think I'd better not be seen with you."

He told Joseph of the threatening phone call to Mrs.
Helga—the reason she had entrusted Henry with getting
the documents to the solicitor. Joseph, bewildered, asked
whether Henry put any credence at all in the phone call.
Henry simply could not say. There had been, it was true,
several hoax telephone calls. There had also been one
murder.

The solicitor looked worried. The sooner he saw the
police, he muttered, the better. And the sooner he found
the Stella will, the better. He doubted if Carl had de-
posited it in his local bank, or the bank would have
been in touch with the police, and with Joseph himself,
before now. Presumably, therefore, if Coppock didn't

have it, it would be somewhere among Carl Grossman's private papers, either in his office or his house.

"Let us hope, for the lovely Stella's sake," said Henry mischievously, "that it wasn't in Carl Grossman's desk."

Joseph stared at him for a moment, then took the implication.

"Don't, Henry," he begged. "You'll give me a thrombosis!"

Henry stood himself an excellent lunch at his club. He supposed he would have to return to the Royal Albert by evening, but at least he would do so with one decent meal inside him for the day.

At the club table he happened to sit next to Ronnie James.

"I see from the *Post*," said Ronnie, "that Kate is covering another murder case. It's no job for a woman. Why do you let her do it?"

"Do you know any way of making Kate do as she's told?"

He knew that, before she married him, Kate had turned Ronnie James down. Sometimes she joked about it. If she had married Ronnie, she would by now have been an MP's wife, instead of having to slave away as a newspaper reporter to help keep an indigent lawyer in the style to which he aspired. In moments of irritation, the joke became a little sharper.

"A great girl," sighed Ronnie, "but, I have to admit, a will of iron—and dubious taste in men."

Henry dutifully laughed.

They talked of this and that throughout the meal. As Ronnie James was rising to go, he said, "By the way, did you know that fellow who got killed—what'sisname?"

"Carl Grossman."

"Ah, yes. Did Kate know he was staying at Smith's Hotel over the weekend, and there was some sort of a shindy?"

"She knew he was at the hotel with his PA, but not about any shindy. What happened?"

"Is the PA a somewhat hippy-looking young fellow?"

"I believe so. Philip Sutton his name is. I haven't met him, but Kate describes him like that."

"He was probably the one, then. It seems that, on Sunday night, he and Grossman had a flaming row. I was having a drink at Smith's yesterday, and Freddie, the barman, told me all about it. They're all a bit intrigued to have had a murder victim actually staying in the place the night before he got done."

"What about the row?"

"It was upstairs in Grossman's room. Seems he has a suite permanently booked for him in the hotel. There was a lot of shouting and commotion, and other guests complained. In the end, the manager had to go up and ask Grossman to pipe down—very embarrassing, have to tick off one of your best customers."

"Does anybody know what the row was about?"

"I suppose Freddie could tell you that, if anyone could. You know Freddie?"

"Known him for years. I'll stroll round to Smith's and have a word with him. Thanks, Ronnie."

"Glad to be of help. Love to Kate."

Smith's Hotel stood only a block away. Freddie worked in the back bar, the intimate one, entered through a rear entrance, which most of the hotel guests never discovered; they used the big cocktail bar off the front lobby. For the familiars, Freddie was even more of an institution than the quaint, discreet little hotel itself. He was a short, spare, witty Cockney, originally from somewhere around the docks, who was said to have been told more family secrets by young gentlemen in their cups than anyone else in Mayfair—and he never betrayed a confidence.

There were only two customers in the bar, talking quietly to each other at one end; on a hot day in August, trade was inevitably slack.

Freddie welcomed Henry with a smile of pleasure. "Good afternoon, Mr. Theobald."

"Afternoon, Freddie. Something long and cool—iced lager, I think."

He knew better than to offer Freddie one; in that bar, a solecism. He led up by asking Freddie for his opinion of Kate's stories in the *Post*. Freddie was enthusiastic. Did Mr. Theobald know, by the way, that Mr. Grossman had actually been staying at Smith's the night before he was murdered? Henry did know.

"Mr. James was telling me," he said, "that there was a row of some kind."

"There was a bit of trouble, sir. Mr. Grossman had his personal assistant staying with him."

"Philip Sutton."

"Ah, you know Mr. Sutton, sir? Mr. Grossman had a permanent suite in the hotel—a sitting-room, bathroom and two bedrooms—which he used when he came to London on business. He has had it for two or three years. Mr. Sutton was staying with him. On Sunday evening there was a lot of shouting in the suite and another guest complained. Of course, directly he was told of the complaint, Mr. Grossman apologized and the noise stopped."

"But you're sure he and Sutton were having a row?"

"So it seems, sir. Mr. Sutton left early on Monday morning. Mr. Grossman was here for another twenty-four hours."

"Do you know what the row was about?"

Freddie, polishing a row of glasses standing on the rear of the bar, shook his head. "I don't think anybody knows that—except, of course, Mr. Sutton."

"Probably not much to it, anyway."

"Probably not, sir," agreed Freddie, busy with his cloth and the next glass. It was nearly closing time.

Henry took a bus to Chelsea and climbed the stairs to his flat. He would pick up fresh clothes for them both. It was tempting to think of staying one more night in London, but he sighed to himself, aware that he would have to go back to help Kate. Besides, he had this interesting snippet of news from the hotel to tell her. Provided she got Sutton's side of the story too, she could use that.

Henry would also give her a general idea of the facts he had learned from Bill Joseph about the Grossman will. But that would have to be background information only, until the will was read and the police agreed to make any relevant provisions known. Whether they would release anything publicly about Grossman's intention to make a fresh will, Henry doubted. Joseph would tell them of it, of course. And it was thought-provoking. A changed will, or a threatened change, could certainly suggest a motive for murder. Henry would have to think that out carefully and lengthily.

He had just finished packing the clothes into a bag when the phone rang.

"Hallo, Henry. It's Butch. I've been trying to reach you for an hour. I missed you at your club, so I've been ringing your flat every fifteen minutes."

"I was having a drink at Smith's. What's up?"

"Nothing to be alarmed about. Kate's quite all right."

"Come on, Butch. Tell me straight."

"She was being shown round the labs at Grossman Electronics, and there was an accidental explosion. She's not hurt. Young Hayward pushed her down behind a blast-wall . . ."

"Blast-wall? What the hell . . . ?"

"It seems they're on defence work that entails explosive devices. Their chief scientist, Dr. Luxton, took them round the labs. He was testing for safety when he got a warning signal—in time to shout to Kate and Hayward to take cover. Kate is all right. Geoff Hayward saw to that. He himself was incredibly lucky. A splinter from the bomb, or whatever it was, actually grazed the back of his scalp as he ducked. Dr. Luxton, who was nearer and not so well protected, got a broken arm and was carted off to hospital with concussion."

Henry was muttering oaths into the phone. "You must take her off the job, Butch. It's getting too damn dangerous."

"Can you see Kate giving it up now?"

"Order her to."

"Be reasonable, Henry. Calm down. This was an accident. It isn't going to happen again, and there's nothing sinister about it. Kate assured me of that when she phoned. Naturally, she has hit it up a bit in her story for the paper. She has done a great piece."

"To hell with the paper. Did she sound all right?"

"A bit shaken," Butch admitted. "She asked me to find you, and get you back to her as soon as possible. You've left your car with her, so I'll send an office car to take you."

"How does Kate know it was only an accident?"

"You'd better ask her."

"Oh, get stuffed," said Henry irritably, "and send that car."

CHAPTER 11

In the lobby of the Royal Albert he was stopped by Geoff Hayward, who had been waiting for him.

"Is she all right?"

"Yes, quite all right. But the doctor insisted she should take a sedative and spend the rest of the day in bed. He said she might get delayed shock." Geoff grinned. "She wouldn't do it until she had dictated a story to the *Post* —a great story. She's a grand person, Henry."

Henry nodded, still anxious. "Butch told me you pushed her to safety as the thing exploded. It seems inadequate just to say thank you. And you nearly bought it yourself, he said. I see you've got the back of your head plastered."

"Nothing to worry about. A piece of metal grazed the skin, that's all."

"If you'd been a fraction of a second slower . . ."

"Ah well,' remarked Geoff, grinning again, "I wasn't."

"I'll go up and see how she is," said Henry.

She stirred when he eased open the bedroom door. "Hallo, darling. Don't fuss. I'm all right."

He leaned over the bed to kiss her cheek gently. Her colour was normal, he was relieved to note. She did not seem upset, just sleepy.

"Don't talk," he said softly. "I've looked in to see if you want anything."

"Nothing, darling. Too sleepy. The doc gave me a whacking great pill."

"I'll be in the sitting-room. I'll leave the bedroom door ajar, so that you can call if you need me. Later I'll go down to the bar for a sandwich. Do you want anything to eat?"

"No. They brought me a cup of tea. Nothing else."

He bent over the bed to kiss her again. "Now just sleep. We'll talk in the morning."

As he went out, she murmured, so sleepily and softly that he barely heard her, "Talk in the morning. But it wasn't an accident."

In the morning it was she who woke him. "Wake up, Henry. There'll be a lot to do. Ring for breakfast, darling, and the papers."

While they were coming, she took her bath. Henry sat on the edge of the bed, yawning. She seemed quite recovered, fresh as ever; she was singing her usual tuneless songs in the bath. Henry yawned again. What energy! Then he sighed, plugged in his razor and shaved. When the maid arrived with the breakfast tray, he told her to set it on the table on the balcony. The day was already heating up, the sunshine already dazzling. He slanted the big umbrella to shade the table.

Kate came out, still damp, wrapped only in a bath-sheet, with a towel turban-style round her head. When she was seated, she pulled off the towel and shook down her hair to dry in the sun.

"I don't know what that stuff was the doctor gave me," she told Henry, "but I feel wonderful."

"You'll feel even better when you've looked at the papers."

She reached for the pile, taking the *Post* first. The explosion in the factory was front-page in all of them, but none, naturally, could have a story as good as hers. Kate gave a satisfied smile. "They've done me proud."

"You've done them proud," said Henry, "and I'm damned worried. I wish you'd let somebody else take over now, Kate. You've done more than your share. It's getting too dangerous."

"If you think I'm going to give up a peach of a story like this, you must be dotty."

"It's not worth such risks. I met Ronnie James at the club yesterday, and he was saying the same."

"That fuddy-duddy!" she scorned.

"Seriously, darling. You yourself said last night that the explosion was no accident. Why do you think it wasn't, by the way?"

"Just listen to this," said Kate, "and see what you think."

She gave him the details of her visit to Grossman Electronics. "To call that an accident is to assume a wild coincidence, wouldn't you say?"

"You mean, it was done to cover up the theft of the booby-trap that killed Grossman?"

"Exactly. Whoever stole it knew that Grossman had locked up the room, and nobody else would open it until Dr. Luxton got there. He must have known, of course, that Luxton was away sick, and the boobytrap must have been stolen after Grossman left last Friday afternoon. Whoever stole it knew there was a test routine that Luxton would go through when he opened up. So he altered something or other to set off a bomb in the blast-chamber from which the thing had been stolen. The explosion would destroy everything else in that blast-chamber, so nobody could tell what, if anything, had been removed from it previously. There were several booby-traps set up on all the benches.

Henry considered. "That would imply that whoever stole the device that killed Grossman—presumably the same person who murdered him—had enough technical knowledge to fiddle something in the circuits of the blast-chamber to ensure an explosion when the test routine was operated. I wonder if it's possible to tell how much expertise the chap would have to have."

"Dr. Luxton would know. But yesterday he was unconscious, and then sedated. Directly the works open I must ring Vera to find out how the old boy is. He's a pleasant man, Dr. Luxton. I liked him."

Henry interrupted. "Just a minute. There was no need for the thief to have rigged up an explosion to hide his theft. You said that Luxton himself told you he didn't know how many of the devices Grossman exploded when he was working there last Friday morning—and any record would almost certainly have been destroyed."

"It's an objection," agreed Kate, "but not a sound one. The thief wouldn't have known that. At least, he couldn't have been sure. Grossman might have told Luxton exactly what he had been doing. They did talk on the phone that morning. The only safe way of hiding the theft was to blow up everything on the bench, in what would seem like an accident."

"Maybe. But I won't be convinced until we get technical confirmation from Luxton. The works'll be open in a few minutes. Ring Vera while I get my bath. Find out how Luxton is."

When he emerged again she had made the call.

"He's much better, I'm glad to say. His arm's in plaster, but the concussion was only slight. When he came round last night, Roger Wake went to the hospital to see him. And he told Dr. Luxton not to talk to anybody about what had happened—especially not to me, Vera says, or to you. Cheek!"

Henry laughed. "Never mind. Let me tell you what I came across in London."

When he had finished, Kate whistled softly. "Darling, we've got almost too much."

"Let's take them one by one."

"Take whom?"

"The suspects. I'll try to sum each one up. You make notes."

"Okay," she agreed, reaching for a pad of copy-paper from the side table.

"Start with Stella Grossman," began Henry. "Her motive's terrific. Grossman had left her a large fortune in his will, and was about to cut her out of it."

"It's a motive only if she knew that."

"Granted. But there had been a row between them. That's a fair assumption. What about? There's gossip that Stella was having an affair with Philip Sutton. Remember our three types of motive—sex, greed, secrets. Stella seems pretty well involved in the first two."

"Do you think," asked Kate, "that the affair between Stella and Philip was enough to make Grossman change his will? Jealous husband? Seems a bit thin, these days."

"How about jealous boyfriend? Carl Grossman's in love with Philip, and finds that Stella has seduced him. How about that? Carl had the reputation of being a vindictive man when crossed. A homosexual whose wife steals his partner . . . Could be."

Kate was gazing at him. "I didn't realize that you had that sort of mind, darling."

Henry smiled sweetly at her. "There are, perhaps, depths in me, which, etc. But back to Stella. There's one big snag. Whoever set the trap for Grossman had to have access to the explosives lab, at some time during the weekend, or on Monday night. It doesn't seem likely that Stella had. Her arrival at the works when they were closed would have been so unusual, surely, that somebody must have known about it. And they haven't told the police."

"Perhaps whoever it was is in cahoots with Stella. Perhaps she had a partner to do the dirty work for her."

"You mean Philip, of course. If he and Stella have joined, he certainly had motive. The likelihood is that he knew Grossman intended to alter his will. He and Grossman had a furious row in the hotel on the Sunday night. It seems probable that, in his anger, Grossman told him he would cut his wife off from his money. If you take her, he shouts—or perhaps, if she takes you—the pair of you can bugger off (if you'll pardon the inexactitude) and fend for yourselves. Next morning Grossman starts to carry out his threat. He calls on his solicitor and tells him to draft a fresh will, leaving nothing at all to Stella. But if Grossman should happen to die before that will were executed, she gets the fortune. And if she and Philip . . . It fits, you know. Moreover, Philip had opportunity. He came back to the works a day before Grossman. Even if Grossman's bunch of factory keys was locked in his desk,

Philip probably knew where to get hold of the duty-room key to the explosives lab, or possibly how to filch Arthur Coppock's key. It would be interesting to know if Philip stayed at the office after working hours last Monday."

"Unless he tells us, how can we know?"

"We could pass over to the police what I heard in London. They'll get most of it from Bill Joseph anyway—have probably talked to him already, And perhaps, in return . . ."

Kate laughed. "Not Mr. Wake, I assure you."

"We ought to pass the information to him anyway."

"Let me have a chance at Philip first," she begged.

When he doubtfully consented, she hastily changed the subject. "What other suspects?"

"Are there any more?"

"Young Terry Jenkins."

"Do you consider him seriously? He had plenty of opportunity, but no motive that we know of. I suppose he might have been able to get hold of a key to the explosives lab. He had some knowledge of and skill at electrical circuits—enough, probably, not only to have fixed the boobytrap under Grossman's desk, but to have fiddled the wires in the blast-chamber to cause an explosion when Dr. Luxton came to do the routine tests. By the way, we've nothing to indicate that Philip Sutton had any such technical ability."

"One point in favour of Philip. Anybody else?"

"There's one man, of course, who had more opportunity than anybody. Arthur Coppock himself. He had a key to the explosives room. Nobody would have questioned, or even much noticed, his movements around the building. After all those years in control of the firm, he must have picked up rudimentary knowledge of the products, and the techniques."

"But no motive."

"There might be," argued Henry. "We simply don't know. He might have been cooking the books, for instance, and Grossman found out. There could be plenty of motives inside the firm. We don't have the facts."

"What you're forgetting," Kate pointed out, "is that there was a telephoned warning of the bomb in the factory. He could hardly have managed that without an accomplice."

"Of course he could. What's more, it's the most convincing point against Coppock," declared Henry triumphantly. "The man who was usually so punctual was ten minutes late that morning. The phone call came during that time. On his way in, he had simply to stop at a callbox and make the call. Vera Sanderson answered it. She said the voice was muffled, disguised, as though the man were speaking through a handkerchief or a scarf. If it were Coppock, he would have to disguise his voice, or the girl would certainly have recognized it."

"The same applies to Philip."

Henry admitted that it did, even if not with quite so much force. But then he suddenly remembered his talk with Mrs. Helga. She had received a threatening phonecall later on the day of the murder. She too said the voice was disguised. "But she said that, at first, she thought it was Arthur Coppock. Then she added that it couldn't have been, for reasons which she wouldn't tell me. I think Mr. Coppock is coming out among the front runners."

Kate was sitting quietly, pondering. "We're overlooking the major factor—the oddest."

"The hoaxes."

"Exactly. When you think of the hoaxes, none of what we've been saying makes much sense. To start with, they completely eliminate Arthur Coppock. He was on the receiving end of one of them—the poison-in-the-paste hoax. And why should any of the people we've mentioned work up a series of stupid hoaxes leading up to one that turns out to be genuine murder? Why, Henry, why? You yourself said that was the key to the whole thing, and that if we could find out why we should probably discover who."

He had to admit it. The links with Grossman were such that they must have been part of the murder plan. They seemed senseless, but they could not have been. They must have had a purpose.

"Still, Kate, we haven't got the least idea what that purpose was. So it seems to me we'll have to fall back on the cases we've been arguing against our various suspects."

"So we follow them up?" she asked.

"I can't see anything else to do. And we might in the process get a clue to the hoaxes."

"Do you think you could tackle Arthur Coppock, Henry? If it's financial, I'm out of my depth."

"I doubt if I could get anything out of him," he answered. "He seems altogether too shrewd a gent. But I might be able to find out more if I went back to Mrs. Helga. I could say I was reporting on my mission to the solicitor."

"You do that, darling," agreed Kate. "I'll go after Philip Sutton—but indirectly. I'll try for Stella."

CHAPTER 12

There was no repetition of the delay when Henry rang Mrs. Helga Grossman's doorbell. The door was opened straight away by a stocky man of about thirty, with a strong facial resemblance to the old woman.

"Yes?"

"You would be Mr. George Grossman, I expect," began Henry pleasantly. "I've come to see your mother. My name's Theobald. She asked me to take something to her solicitors, and I've come to tell her that this has been done."

"I'll tell her," said the man, starting to close the door.

But the woman's strong, deep voice came from beyond him. "Bring Mr. Theobald in, Georg."

Reluctantly the man opened the door again and jerked with his head to enter.

Helga Grossman was seated as before in the heavy, sombre room. She took Henry's greeting and motioned him to a chair. Her son sat himself on an upright chair by the wall and gazed closely at Henry.

"I delivered the documents to Mr. Joseph as you asked me to, Mrs. Grossman. He was a bit taken aback, of course. He wanted to come to see you, but I told him the prudent course would be to get in touch with the police, without approaching you in person."

"Mr. Joseph telephoned me," she told Henry. "He saw the police yesterday, and he has an appointment with Mr. Coppock for today. Then he will telephone me again. The police inspector also came to see me."

"When?" demanded her son suddenly. "And what about?"

"Last evening, when you had gone out, Georg."

"Why didn't you tell me?"

"It is no concern of yours."

The man stared suspiciously from one to the other. Then he asked, in a gruff voice, "What's this all about? What documents? What's the solicitor got to do with it?"

Helga Grossman hesitated. Henry murmured gently that the facts were bound to become public soon.

"Very well," she decided. "Tell him."

Henry turned to face George Grossman directly. "At your mother's request, I took her marriage certificate, and other documents relating to her marirage, to her solicitor, for safe keeping."

George was staring at him. "Why?"

"They showed that your mother married Carl Grossman in Hamburg in 1938."

"Uncle Carl?" He swung round to his mother. "You were married to Uncle Carl? Then there was a divorce."

"There was no divorce."

"But my father . . . Are you saying that Carl was not my uncle, but my father?"

"No, George. Carl was my husband, but not your father. Carl left Germany in 1938. So it is evident he was not your father."

"I don't understand," he growled. "You mean you lived with Carl's brother in Germany, and I . . ."

"Carl had no brother."

"I demand an explanation," he said suddenly. "I am entitled to an explanation."

The woman's voice hardened. "Later. It is not necessary to discuss this with Mr. Theobald. Later we will talk. Now, remain silent."

Slightly to Henry's surprise, George obeyed, leaning back in his chair, sullen, but quiet. Evidently his mother still had a command of him, when she wished to have.

Henry asked, "Did Mr. Joseph tell you about Carl's will when he telephoned?"

Helga shook her head. "What about Carl's will?"

"The whole thing could prove very difficult. Carl called

on the solicitor on Monday, when he was in London, and
gave him instructions to launch Grossman Electronics as
a public company. It could scarcely have been done before next year. He also told him to prepare, for his con-
sideration, the draft of a new will, leaving his shares in
the company to a charitable trust. As you told me, Carl
had already discussed this with you, and you wouldn't
join in the trust."

"Now it no longer matters," she said.

"In a sense it does. Carl's previous will must now get
probate. That, I understand, leaves his shares in the
company to Stella. If that will is not challenged, therefore, you and she will own most of the company. Of
course, she must face very heavy estate duty. I don't know
whether Carl had made any provision for that. If not,
Stella will certainly have to sell a substantial part of her
shareholding. I'm sure Mr. Joseph will advise her to go
ahead with Carl's proposal to float the company publicly.
Then the shares would get a Stock Exchange quotation
and could be sold, at any time, at the market price." He
noticed she was looking grim. "Wouldn't you agree, Mrs.
Grossman? You couldn't stop such a scheme if it were
pressed, because you don't have a deciding vote. But as
the second-largest shareholder, owning one-fifth of the
company, your views would carry a lot of weight. I think,
if you want my opinion, that you would be well advised
to agree."

"I am not the second-largest shareholder," she said in
a low voice. "Arthur Coppock is."

"You are registered as such," Henry pointed out. Then
he understood. "You mean that you have pledged your
shareholding, or part of it, to Mr. Coppock, for a con-
sideration."

Helga slowly inclined her head. "Some years ago."

Henry said comfortingly, "That need not matter. All
you have to do is repay the money you borrowed and
the shares remain yours. That is not a difficult financial
transaction. Even if you no longer have the money, Mr.
Joseph could easily arrange the matter with your bank."

She was looking ever grimmer. "It was part of the bargain that Arthur Coppock has an option to buy my shares at any time."

Henry was startled. "At an agreed price?"

"An agreed price."

"A low price?"

"It was part of the bargain."

Her son burst in angrily, "You did that? You must have been crazy."

She gazed hard at him. "Yes, Georg, I was crazy. I did it for you."

"For me? You said you would get the money from Carl."

"Would you have cared," she asked curtly, "where it came from?"

He leaned back in his chair, silent, his face colouring angrily.

Trying to cool things, Henry remarked that it was doubtless something on which Mr. Joseph would advise her. The legal position might not be what she imagined it was. He supposed she had some papers about it, some record.

Helga slowly shook her head. "I signed a paper. Arthur took it away when he gave me the money."

"Have you been receiving the dividends on your shares?"

"Yes, but . . ."

"But you paid interest on the loan?" Henry guessed. "Heavy interest? How heavy?"

"A proportion of the dividend." She hesitated, then added, "Half. But I have to pay tax on the whole."

'Good lord!" murmured Henry. It was as nasty a spot of usury as he could recall. She had been pretty nearly skinned; left just enough to keep herself going—or, of course, there might have been trouble, revelations. He was speedily forming a definite impression of this astute business man, Arthur Coppock, whom he must certainly meet.

Helga broke in with a question. "This will, leaving

Carl's shares to Stella—since I am his true wife, can I not fight it?"

"Certainly. Mr. Joseph will advise you about that, I am sure."

"And if I won . . . ?"

"It would be a long and expensive law suit, Mrs. Grossman. But in the very odd, unusual circumstances, you might win, either wholly, or substantially. Then the shares, or whatever fraction of them the court decided, would be yours. But I expect Mr. Joseph would advise you to try to settle the matter out of court, to come to a compromise with Stella, taking part of the shares each."

He was astonished by the sudden look of agony—or was it rage?—in her eyes. He tried to recall his exact words. He must go over them carefully, at leisure, to see if he could discern what it was he had said that could possibly have hurt, or angered her.

As he passed the entrance to the Oliver Twist bar on his way up to his rooms—the bar already crowded with reporters in a before-lunch session—Henry noticed Bill Joseph sitting at the far end. He elbowed up to him. "Still here?"

"Yes, there are complications. Have a drink?"

"This bar's too crowded, and mostly with newspapermen. I've a sitting-room upstairs. Come up and have a drink there."

"Gladly," said Joseph.

He was immensely impressed with the Pickwick Suite. "I suppose you don't want a lodger?" he facetiously inquired as he settled comfortably on the balcony with a large gin. "All I could get last night was an attic at the back of the hotel, with a fine view of the gasworks."

"Well, it is a seaside resort in August, Bill. And the murder has brought Fleet Street down in strength."

"The sooner I can get back to London and civilization, the happier I shall be. But heaven knows when."

"Complications, you said. About Grossman's will?"

"We can't find it."

"He told you he gave it for safe keeping to Arthur Coppock."

"Coppock says he didn't. Coppock didn't even know he'd made a will, he says. He assumed he had, of course, and that it was lodged with us."

"Do you believe him?"

"I see no reason not to, Henry. It doesn't affect him, one way or the other. And he's a very methodical, orderly man of business, and quite co-operative. He offered to open all his files for a search. I think Chief Superintendent Roger Wake may take him up on that. It has such an obvious bearing on motive."

"It must turn up," was Henry's opinion. "A man with a million to leave doesn't carelessly lose his will—not even such an unpredictable man as Carl Grossman."

"Well, it isn't in his bank. Coppock hasn't got it. Stella Grossman, who stands to benefit most from it, had never seen it. Her only knowledge of it is that Carl, whenever in a temper, used to threaten to cut her out of it. Other than that, she knows nothing of it. A preliminary look through the house hasn't revealed it. I've phoned for a couple of my clerks to get down here fast, to make a thorough search of all papers, in the house, and in the offices. I don't think the will is in either. What I hope is that they'll turn up a receipt for a safe-deposit somewhere, in which Carl had stowed it. My nightmare is that awful joke you made—suppose it was in the desk that was destroyed by the bomb!"

"If it doesn't turn up in the statutory period," said Henry, "and those German documents are proved genuine, Helga will inherit under an intestacy, I take it."

"Let's not cross bridges until we come to them," begged Joseph. He gladly held out his glass for Henry to refill it.

"I assume you've told Stella that she isn't Mrs. Grossman," said Henry.

Joseph looked uncomfortable. "I intended to. But the superintendent asked me to say nothing of it until he let me know. You see my problem, Henry—duty as a solici-

tor to my client clashing with duty as a citizen to the police. But I certainly can't keep Stella in the dark for long.
Still, Helga herself will probably break the deadlock."

"I was with her this morning," Henry told him, "and I
found out how she raised that £10,000. She didn't make
an actual reference to it, but I'm sure it's what she was
talking about. She pledged her shares, plus 50 per cent of
the dividends before tax, and an option to buy the shares
at any time at an agreed price. She didn't tell me the price,
but admitted it was low."

Joseph whistled. "What idiots people are to pass up
their lawyers and go to moneylenders."

"Your father passed her up," Henry reminded him,
"on Carl's instructions."

"True. Did she go to a licensed man? She could get
him under the Moneylenders' Act."

"It was a private arrangement," said Henry.

"With whom? Do you know?"

"With that methodical man of business who is being so
co-operative with you, Arthur Coppock."

Bill Joseph put down his glass, staring with astonishment. "Do the police know?"

"I doubt it. But I reckon we ought to tell them."

CHAPTER 13

Kate was just leaving the Royal Albert when the hall porter called to her. "Mrs. Theobald. Telephone." She took it in the booth round the corner from the desk. It was Geoff Hayward.

"Roger Wake is up at the Grossman factory."

"What's he after?"

"I'm not sure. One of the chaps got hold of Kippis, who said it was a routine check-up. But according to our friend, Wake has something to work on, and he's definitely after somebody—we don't know who. Most of the lads know of the visit by now, and they're hanging around to try to get something from the super when he comes out."

"I don't think they'll get much," said Kate. "But you'd better cover it, Geoff, just in case. Keep in touch here. I've a call of my own to make, but I expect I'll be back here this afternoon."

Since Henry had taken the car, she picked up a taxi to Warnham Court. The place looked deserted. She rang several times, but nobody came to the door. So she told the taxi driver to park over on the other side of the drive, and walked round to the back of the house. It was obviously still being used, for some of the upper windows were open. Kate mounted wide stone steps to the terrace and peered through the tall french windows into a huge drawing-room, beautifully furnished. The piano was a concert grand, yet it seemed scarcely to fill one end of the room. Nobody was there. She walked hesitatingly along the terrace. The other set of windows displayed a dining-room with a large mahogany table, bare of ornament, but the chairs placed correctly around it. The walls were closely hung with oils, some of them, she guessed, immensely good. But there was nobody in that room either.

The silence, and the emptiness, began to edge into her nerves. She peered over the stone balustrade at the end of the terrace. The kitchen outbuildings lay to that side of the house, but to reach them she would have to go back to the wide stone steps. At the top of them she paused to gaze around; first the lawns, edged with roses and belts of shrubs and trees; at the far end of the lawns, a line of white railings; beyond, parkland on which sheep and a few heifers were grazing under the shade of occasional trees; then a line of willows marking the course of the river.

"Can I help you, miss?" came a man's voice behind her.

Kate turned, startled. She had not heard him approach. He was evidently a gardener, trowel in hand, trousers hitched below the knee.

"I am looking for Mrs. Grossman."

"Ah, she's in the summerhouse." He pointed, and Kate noticed for the first time a small wooden chalet set among the trees, facing towards the river. "Is she expecting you, Miss?"

"No, I don't think so. But it's rather important that I see her. Don't let me bother you. I'll go down to the summerhouse."

The gardener looked at her uncertainly, but did not try to stop her when she walked firmly down the steps and across the lawn. When she glanced back, he had already turned aside and was working on the Italian pots of geranium and lobelia spaced at intervals long the balustrade.

The summerhouse was a small building of modern design with big glass windows in front and a paved patio facing towards the river. Stella Grossman, in a black bikini and large green sun-glasses, lay on a brightly-coloured garden couch on the patio. She had a lovely body, smaller than Kate remembered, but exquisite. Her long dark hair, fastened into a ponytail, stretched across the blue and scarlet cushion.

At first Kate thought she was asleep. But then, without moving, she spoke. "You're the woman from the newspaper, aren't you? What do you want?"

Kate sat in a deckchair, pulling the canopy over to shade her face from the sun, but also putting on her own dark glasses, partly to lessen the glare, but chiefly to get on equal terms with Stella Grossman.

"I thought you might like to be kept in touch with what is happening, Mrs. Grossman. The police superintendent is at your factory now. I think he has gone there to question Mr. Sutton."

The woman's face did not move, and the sun-glasses hid any change in expression. But her fingers tautened against the cushions on which her hands were resting. Her voice, when she spoke, was languid. But there had been a short pause while she made it so.

"Philip? Really? What should they want to question Philip about?"

"Perhaps about his quarrel with your husband in Smith's Hotel on Sunday night. You knew there was a quarrel?"

"Yes, I knew."

"And what it was about?"

The woman remained silent, immobile.

"Or perhaps," Kate went on after a pause, "about his movements on Monday." When there was still no response, she added, "You do see the implication, don't you? After a loud quarrel on Sunday night, Mr. Sutton returned to the factory on Monday morning. He could probably have had easy access to the laboratory where the boobytraps were stowed. He had better access than anybody else to Carl Grossman's office. The probability is that the explosive device was fixed to the desk at some time during the day—most likely, after the factory had closed for the night. So I suppose the superintendent might be asking Mr. Sutton why he stayed on for a while before leaving that evening."

For the first time Stella's expression changed. She smiled. "Then the answer should satisfy the superintendent. He did not stay after the factory closed. He was there for a while on Monday morning, but not at all in the afternoon."

"You mean," asked Kate, "that he was elsewhere?"

"He was here, with me. Here in the summerhouse. We had lunch together here, and he did not return to the factory. Does that satisfy your curiosity, Mrs. Theobald?"

Kate politely nodded. But in truth it did not satisfy, but rather enlarged her curiosity. She looked along the belt of shrubs and trees that ran to the river bank. At the end stood a small white gate, evidently leading to a riverside path. Then she glanced through the window into the summerhouse. It was furnished with a table, chairs, a bed. So did Philip Sutton always use that footpath to come unobtrusively to the summerhouse? And did Stella Grossman, like a modern Madame Bovary, steal across the lawn from the house, to meet her lover there? And had Carl Grossman found out? Was that the simple answer?

But, of course, it could not be. How about the hoaxes? They could not, surely, be fitted into any ordinary triangular tale; certainly not into that of a quarrel which took place only two days before the murder, and well after the hoaxes had been perpetrated.

Then the white gate opened, and a man came through, hastening towards the summerhouse. Philip Sutton.

As he approached, Kate saw how distressed he looked, almost distraught. He hesitated for a moment when he caught sight of Kate, but then came on, holding out his hands towards Stella, catching hers when she raised them, dropping on to his knees beside her. "They've been questioning me for more than an hour. The police. That awful superintendent—cold, polite, efficient. I swear he thinks I'm the man."

Stella moved her head slightly in Kate's direction, warning.

Philip swivelled towards her, then released Stella's hands, rose from his crouch, pulled over a chair to sit in. "Oh, but I'm glad you're here. I've been talking to Geoff Hayward. He says you've reported other murder cases, and actually found the murderers."

"I've helped a little, perhaps."

"Then help me. Mrs. Theobald, help me. You don't know how badly I need help. That policeman—I thought at one moment that he was going to charge me this morning."

"Charge you?"

"With Carl's murder."

"Because of your row with him at Smith's Hotel on Sunday night? Surely he'd need more than that."

"You know about that?" he asked.

"It wasn't exactly a secret row, Mr. Sutton—or so I'm told."

He was staring at her absently, as though his thoughts were on something else. "If that were all!"

"What else is there?" she asked. When he remained silent, she repeated, "What else is there, Mr. Sutton?" After another pause she said quietly, "You asked just now for my help. If you meant it, you must be open with me."

"Be careful, Philip," Stella suddenly intervened.

But he shook his head at her. "She's right, Stella. If I want her to help me, I must tell her. I went into the explosives lab at the factory on Monday morning. Oh, don't look startled. It was quite ordinary, and quite innocent. Carl had asked me to. When we were in London on Saturday he remembered that he had left his explosives log, and several folders of notes, on one of the benches when he locked the place up on Friday morning, after working there. He told me to get them up when we returned to the

works. I am his PA. I was always running errands like
that for him."

"How did you get into the lab?" asked Kate.

"With Carl's key."

"Dr. Luxton told me that Carl always kept his factory
keys locked in his office desk."

"So he did, usually. But we left in a bit of a hurry on
Friday afternoon, and he put them by mistake into his
travelling bag. It was when he opened the bag in the
hotel on Saturday that he found the bunch and remembered he had left his notes on the bench. He made a joke
about his failing memory, and threw the keys across to
me, telling me to get the notes when we got back. He
joked that he was getting so old that he was certain to
forget. So I put the keys in my briefcase. Then, on Monday morning, I went to the lab and fetched the notes."

"Even after the row?" she asked.

"Why not? The row had nothing to do with it. The row
was personal. I was still his PA, still his employee. I still
had to carry out his instructions as part of my work."

Kate asked, "How did the police know you had been
there?"

"Arthur Coppock happened to be passing the lab door
when I came out. He remembered it only this morning,
and of course he had to tell the police. I'm not blaming
Arthur at all. The superintendent asked him if I had
been carrying anything. Arthur said he hadn't really
noticed, but his recollection was that I had something,
but he couldn't say what. Of course, he was right. I was
carrying the folders of notes and the explosives log, tied
up in a parcel, just as Carl had left them on Friday."

Kate asked what he had done with the notes, and he
told her he had put them on Carl's desk. He could not put
them into a drawer, because he had only Carl's factory-
keys bunch, not his desk keys. So he had put the folders
on the desk, together with a lot of other paperwork
awaiting Carl's return. For safety, he had put the factory
keys into his own desk in the adjoining room.

He gazed desperately at Kate. "You can see how this looks to the police," he admitted, almost in despair. "I have a great row with Carl on Sunday night, leave the hotel a day early, come back to the factory, go to the explosives lab where the boobytraps are stored, and I am in and out of Carl's office, on my own, all day Monday. On Tuesday there's a bomb scare which brings him hurrying back from London. Directly he opens his desk, he is killed by a booby-trap from the explosives lab. His key to the lab is in my desk, and the only evidence to support my story that I went to the lab to get his log and notes—the log and the notes themselves—is completely destroyed by the explosion. It's obvious what the police think. But I swear to you it's not so."

Kate reflected. The lab key being in Philip's own desk was probably, she thought, the strongest point in his favour. If he had gone to the lab to get an explosive with which to kill Carl, he would surely have left the keys on Carl's desk, to be discovered after the explosion where they normally should have been.

"How did it happen," she asked, "that Mr. Coppock saw you coming from the lab? What was he doing down there?"

Philip shrugged. "How would I know? There are several store rooms in that basement, and lots of old company files."

For the first time Stella stirred. She raised herself on the couch, swung her feet off on to the floor, shook her head so that her long rope of hair fell across her shoulder and over her breast. The dark glasses hid the expression of her eyes, but her voice was calm enough, clear, almost loud. "I don't think you have impressed Mrs. Theobald very favourably, Philip. She asked you to be frank."

Kate smiled approval. She had not expected an ally there. Philip tried at first to appear puzzled and, when that failed, looked sullen.

"Mrs. Theobald doesn't think your visit to the explosives lab on Monday morning was very important," Stella went on. "You have a perfectly reasonable explanation of it."

"I'll go further," Kate offered. "I'll accept the explanation. And I'll agree with what I am sure Mrs. Grossman is going to say next—that it isn't particularly because of that visit that the police questioned you so lengthily this morning."

"Exactly," said Stella.

"Was it because of your row with Mrs. Grossman," asked Kate, "and what the row was about?"

When Philip remained sullen, silent, the woman took up the thread. "I'll tell you what it was about, Mrs. Theobald. Philip was demanding that Carl should divorce me, so that Philip and I could get married."

Philip's drooping despair seemed confirmation enough.

"Carl refused a divorce," Stella continued. "He said he'd see me in hell first. Have you noticed, Mrs. Theobald, how people in a rage always talk in clichés? Carl was certainly in a rage. It was not losing me he cared about in the least. It was losing Philip."

"Stella, please," he begged. He had dropped his face on to his palms, the fingers covering his eyes.

"You say you are facing a possible charge of murder," she replied in her cold, steady voice. "You say you think this woman from a newspaper can help you to disprove it. Very well, Philip. Then she must have the whole story."

He slowly raised his head, staring first at Stella, then at Kate. He seemed to Kate not to be so frightened now. It was as though the terror had been too much, and he had put it from him.

At last he began to speak. "The whole story," he repeated slowly. "The whole story . . ."

"The facts, anyhow," Kate put in softly.

"Carl and I had a relationship," he said. "You understand?" She nodded. "It meant a great deal to him— more than I ever realized. To me it meant very little, not much more than a bread ticket. You see how I despise myself."

"You were young," put in Stella defensively. "He was rich, brilliant, powerful. He could be immensely attractive. He seduced you, as he had once seduced me."

"Perhaps," muttered the man. "Then I fell in love with Stella—and she, she said, with me. We had to be secret. We were frightened of him. At least, I was. But it was hell. Everything that had happened before nauseated me. I tried to find excuses for not going with him. He was tolerant. I thought even that he didn't care much anyhow. But really he had understood that something had happened, and he was playing discreetly until he found out exactly what."

Stella carried it on. "One afternoon last week he found us here, in this summerhouse, on that bed. He made no attempt to interfere. He said nothing. He just stood there, outside the window, watching. I was the first to see him. We don't even know how long he had been here. When he saw that I had seen him, he turned without a word and went into the house. That evening he took it up with me. He seemed quite calm and cool. He had decided, he said, that I would go on living in his house as long as he lived, but only formally as his wife. He would set up a trust fund that would provide me with a small income after his death, but I was no longer to expect anything from his estate. I told him that I cared very little for his money—which was not, perhaps, absolutely true—but that whether I continued to live in his house depended on what Philip wanted. Carl said he would deal separately with Philip."

As though emboldened by the actual telling of the story, the man seemed stronger now. He told Kate how Carl had ordered him to accompany him to London on Friday, for the customary business trip. They would discuss their personal affair, Carl said, in London. But he kept putting off the discussion. On Friday evening they went to the concert, then back to supper at Smith's. On

Saturday they lunched at the Connaught, and in the evening took in a theatre.

"Every time I tried to talk about Stella, Carl stopped me."

"What did you talk about?" asked Kate.

"Music a good deal, and business matters, of course—plans for the appointments at the Ministry, delays at the factory. Carl was worried about the export deliveries we were missing, largely because of the hoax phone calls. But he thought that would soon be put a stop to."

"He did? How?"

"He was confident that Arthur Coppock would deal with them. He said something about Arthur being pretty sure he knew who the hoaxer was."

"Did he say who?"

"No. I don't think Carl knew whom Arthur had in mind. Anyway, Carl didn't say much about it at all. And I wasn't very interested. All I wanted was to have it out with him about Stella. But he laughed every time I tried, and said that was for later, and started to talk about something else—music, or some general topic. He was charming, amusing, absolutely at his best. And he made no attempt to touch me. On Sunday we went to the cathedral to hear a sung Mass, and went riding in Richmond Park in the afternoon. It was as though nothing had happened to disturb anything.

"Then on Sunday evening, after supper, we settled in his sitting-room at Smith's, with a bottle of whisky, and he said we must now discuss the relationship. He wanted me simply to forget what had occurred, and resume with him. I told him that it was over, and that he must divorce Stella. We wanted to get married. I told him that, whether he divorced her or not, we would go away together.

"He laughed at first, then cajoled, then refused, and suddenly broke into the most awful rage. I've never seen a man so angry. He shouted and raved. I lost my temper and shouted back. In the end, the hotel manager came in, and it had to stop. Carl went to his bedroom without a word. I got up very early next morning and came back to Loxham. That's all there is."

Kate said, "Not quite all, surely. There's the question of the will. Nobody will believe you if you say you're indifferent to that. If Carl Grossman had lived, you would be running off with a penniless woman. Because he died, the woman you are to marry will be very rich indeed—provided, of course, that the will can be found. I gather it hasn't been found yet."

Stella put in, "Whether it is found or not. The solicitor has told me of the difficulty of tracing it. But what difference does it make? If it is found, I understand that I inherit. If it is not, then Carl will have died intestate—the solicitor told me there is no previous will still in existence. So I inherit anyway."

Kate looked at her with astonishment. "The solicitor didn't tell you about Helga Grossman?"

Evidently he had not, for Stella's raised eyebrows seemed genuine interrogation.

"Then perhaps I shouldn't," said Kate. She hesitated. But, after all, it was bound to come out soon. So why not? "Helga married Carl Grossman in Germany just before the war, a short time before he escaped to England."

"Helga married Carl? But Phyllis . . . ?"

"That marriage was bigamous. Carl thought Helga could not have survived. When she turned up in England after the war, he had already married Phyllis. He kept Helga quiet with the bribe of shares in his company."

"When was the divorce?"

"There was no divorce."

Philip Sutton got up quickly, clutched at Kate's shoulder. "You mean, Carl and Stella were not legally married?"

"Helga has documents to prove it. If Carl Grossman is deemed to have died intestate, then I should think that Helga will get his fortune, not Stella. Of course, there may be a legal battle."

Philip Sutton gestured angrily. But it was not he whom

Kate was watching. She was looking covertly at the woman. Because of those damned dark glasses, she could not be sure of her expression. But her lips were trembling, and her hands had gripped hard again, the knuckles white, over the edge of the couch.

CHAPTER 14

When Henry got back to the Royal Albert, Kate was phoning an early story to the *Post*.

"It's all right to use all of it," she was assuring Butch. "I have it from Philip Sutton and Stella Grossman themselves, with their consent. Yes, it's okay. Check on the row at Smith's Hotel if you like, but Henry has already done so. Oh, hallo, darling. No, not you, Butch. It's Henry, he has just come in. Hang on a minute, he's saying something."

She slipped her hand over the telephone mouthpiece.

"You haven't said anything about Helga and the German marriage?" Henry asked, keeping his voice quiet, but anxious.

"No, no. Simply about the row at Smith's, and what Philip Sutton was doing at the factory on Monday morning—I'll tell you about that later—and the missing will. That's all right, surely."

"I'm not sure you should say anything about the will, until Bill Joseph agrees."

"Nonsense, Henry. I got it from Stella Grossman."

"Oh well," he conceded, "in that case . . ."

Kate uncovered the mouthpiece. "It's all right, Butch. Henry just wanted to check on something. He's the nervous type. Everything you've got is okay to use. There's another Press conference at the police station later today, but I don't expect it to turn up anything we haven't already got. Yes, I'll cover it, of course. By the way, one other thing. Among Horace's pictures of the funeral mourners there's one of Helga Grossman—yes, the sister-in-law—and her son George. She uses the German form, Georg. She's holding on to his arm as they leave the village church. George is said to have got mixed up with one of the London criminal outfits some years ago, and then to have gone to Australia. I don't know when he went or when he got back. But see if our chap at Scotland Yard can trace anything about him, will you? And try the cuttings library. What? No, I've nothing definite in mind at all. Just curiosity. Okay, I'll ring you this evening."

When she had hung up, Henry remarked that she seemed to have had some luck with Stella Grossman and Philip Sutton. She gave him an account.

"But I believe him, Henry. I think I believe her too. Only an impression, of course, but I don't think they're the ones. And they don't fit in with the hoaxes."

"Any side issues?"

"Only one. Philip said that, while they were in London, Carl Grossman discussed the delays to the firm's export production, because of the hoaxes. He said that Arthur Coppock was going to deal with it, because Arthur was pretty sure he knew who the hoaxer was."

Henry lowered himself into a chair. "Mr. Coppock again, eh?"

He gave her his interview with Helga and George Grossman.

"The bastard!" murmured Kate. "Have you told Roger Wake?"

"No. Bill Joseph asked me not to, until he had had it out with Coppock himself. Bill is terrified of yet another scandal in his clients' circle."

"Then I think it's time we had another talk with the great-hearted Arthur."

She asked the hotel switchboard to put her through to Grossman Electronics. But Mr. Coppock was in conference with the company's solicitor and could not be disturbed.

"The lawyer's talking to him now," she told Henry.

"We'll have to try him at home this evening. There isn't any time to spare before the Press conference."

As she had expected, the conference yielded nothing new. Sam Kippis conducted it. Roger Wake did not appear. Nothing was said of the missing will, which gratified Kate, since it was a subsidiary lead in her story in the *Post* tomorrow. The inspector confirmed that the device that killed Carl Grossman was a boobytrap removed from a research laboratory in the building; which again gratified her, since she had told that whole story in the *Post* today. All that Kippis would say about the chief superintendent's visit to Grossman Electronics that morning was that he was making routine checks on certain pieces of information which could not be disclosed at present.

Dereck Andrews, who was standing beside Kate, caught the look of mischief in her eyes, and whispered, "Not until tomorrow's edition of the *Post,* eh, Kate?"

But she laughed and told him no comment.

Back in the Royal Albert she was walking through the lobby when she noticed a bulky letter in the Pickwick Suite mail pigeonhole.

"Your second post arrives a bit late, doesn't it?" she asked the porter as he handed it to her.

He glanced at it. "It came by hand, madam. It must be local."

"Did you see who delivered it?"

The porter shook his head. There were so many people moving about in the lobby. Packets were simply left on the reception desk, and when he saw them he sorted them into the pigeonholes.

Upstairs, Kate regarded the packet with suspicion. It was a fairly large, fat, stout brown envelope, addressed to her at the Royal Albert in black block capitals written with a felt nib.

Henry was in the bathroom.

"Henry," she called, "what does a letter-bomb look like?"

He was out at once. He took it from her, handling it gingerly. He found a knife and carefully slit one end of the envelope. Peering inside, he could make out a piece of insulated wire.

"Stay where you are, Kate."

He put the packet on the bathroom floor, closed the door on it and made for the phone, getting through to the police station, asking for Detective-Inspector Kippis.

"Mr. Kippis? Henry Theobald here. My wife has just had delivered to her, by hand at the hotel, what I think may be a letter-bomb . . . Yes, I've put it in our bathroom . . . No, not in water, but on the floor. I'd be glad if you could get someone round rather promptly . . . Yes, thanks."

Kate took the phone. "Come straight up, Inspector, please. We're in the Pickwick Suite, on the second floor. Don't ask for us at the desk. And please try not to be conspicuous. There's one hell of a lot of newspapermen in the bar."

The police car was there in less than three minutes. Kippis came himself, with a plain-clothes man whom he introduced as an explosives expert.

The man went into the bathroom, shut the door, and they waited—waited for what seemed like an hour, but was only about five minutes. Long enough, however, for Henry to hand round strong whiskies. Kate gulped hers. Kippis took his with a nod of thanks.

Then the expert came out of the bathroom, wearing gloves, holding the envelope in one hand, a wad of newspaper tied round with wire in the other.

"Your bomb," he said, grinning.

"What's it about?" asked Kate, bewildered.

Kippis smiled, but sympathetically. "Just another hoax, Mrs. Theobald. But thank heavens your husband called us. This time we've got something actual to work on—the envelope, the newspapers, the wire, the lettering of the address. Up to now, we've had only phone calls, except for the bomb that killed Mr. Grossman." He smiled again. "Mr. Wake hasn't been exactly appreciative of your articles in the *Post*. But, since they've brought us this, he'll be to that extent grateful to you. How was this delivered?"

"It was in our pigeonhole at the reception desk. I saw it when I came back from the Press conference. I don't think it was there when I set out, but I couldn't swear to that. The porter said he didn't notice who delievered it. It was left on the desk. He'll know approximately when."

The expert had carefully wrapped the pieces of the hoax in plastic envelopes and stowed them in his briefcase.

On the point of going, Kippis said, "I'd be obliged if you wouldn't mention this in your newspaper until we've had a chance to get at it, Mrs. Theobald."

"Not tell the story of the hoax played on me—my own personal drama?" she protested.

"I can't compel you. All I can say is that it will materially assist police investigations if you keep silent about it."

"If you promise not to let on to anybody else," she conceded, "I'll hold it for my piece in Monday morning's newspaper."

"That's a deal."

"But if it's in any of the Sundays, Mr. Kippis, watch out for Theobald's Revenge."

He laughed, and went.

Kate gestured to Henry for another scotch. As he handed it to her, the phone rang and she picked it up. "Hallo."

"If you and your husband don't stop prying, it'll be for real next time."

"Who is that?" she demanded sharply. But he had hung up.

She told Henry. He snatched the phone. But all the switchboard girl could remember was that it was from a callbox, asking for Mrs. Theobald.

"Did the voice mean anything to you?" he asked Kate.
She shook her head, but reluctantly. "I don't think so.

For a moment I thought . . . It sounded like a young man. The odd thing is, it was a bit mechanical, as though he were reading a message, or even as though the voice was taped."

"Give Kippis time to get back to the station, then ring and tell him."

"Yes, of course. But, aside from the message, what is there to tell?"

"What you just said."

"If you like," she agreed. "But it can't really mean anything. It's probably only fancy. How can that help?"

They went to bed early. Henry insisted. If she didn't give in, he threatened to call the doctor to give her another pill. She asked, how about dinner? He would phone down to what this hotel laughingly called room service and get something sent up. He recommended ham sandwiches from the bar, which were reasonably edible, and a large jug of coffee. So, after a lapse of time during which Kate had undressed and got into bed, the coffee and sandwiches arrived and they picnicked on them on the bedspread.

"We were going to try to get Arthur Coppock at home and put the Helga questions to him," she pointed out.

"Tomorrow will do."

"Tomorrow is Saturday, darling. I can't write another piece until Sunday for Monday's paper."

"Then tomorrow's our day off," he rejoined. "And Kate, I've an idea. Since we're in a grotty little seaside holiday town, let's have one day's grotty seaside holiday. You know the sort of thing—sea bathing, and lying in the sun on the sands, fish and chips for lunch at a pub on the front, the concert party on the end of the pier, rowing out in a boat to do some sea fishing."

"It's a lovely idea, darling. One day's real seaside holiday, just like mother used to take."

"And you know how a proper holiday begins, Kate?"

"No, I don't, darling," she answered lazily. "You tell me."

"I'll not tell you," said Henry, starting to undress. "I'll show you."

In the morning she was drowsy, but Henry roused her. "Come on, Kate, we're on holiday."

"Lovely," she murmured, "if exhausting."

Stripping back the sheet, he exhorted her, "Bathe in the sea before breakfast on holiday. It'll give you a wonderful appetite. Darling, you look adorable."

"No, Henry," she said firmly, waking now. "Not again. We'll have to have that bathe—nothing like a brisk plunge in cold water, as your housemaster must often have told you."

She slid off the bed, searched hastily for her nightdress, could not find it, avoided Henry's pass at her, and made naked for the bathroom, bolting the door.

To bathe in the sea was simple. They put on their swimsuits, wrapped towels round themselves, and ran from the hotel across the promenade to the beach. There were few people about so early in the morning. The water was wonderfully warm, the tide low and just turning, the sea flat calm and blue under a cloudless sky, more like the Mediterranean than the English Channel. Henry put in a spurt or two, but mostly they swam lazily, or floated blissfully on their backs. By the time they came out, there were already children building sandcastles and family groups forming small colonies with deckchairs.

"I'm hungry," said Kate. "Let's get dressed and have a huge breakfast, and then come and sleep it off in the sun on the beach."

In the hotel dining-room, where breakfast was beginning (and Henry was actually ordering porridge, something he hadn't eaten for years), Dereck Andrews stopped at their table. "Insomnia?"

"Dereck, darling, we're having a seaside holiday. It's our day off."

He grimaced. "It's my day on—the day I have to write something frightfully good. And I haven't got a lead. Can't you spare even a crumb of news for a wretched dog of a Sunday reporter?"

"I used all I have in the *Post* this morning. Can't you follow that up?"

"Somebody in London is checking at Smith's, of course," he told her. "Everybody down here is chasing after Philip Sutton and Stella Grossman. You went a bit far, didn't you, Kate? All that stuff about the demand for a divorce, and his admission that he'd been in the explosives room the day before Carl Grossman copped it. Practically put him in the dock."

"Just what I didn't do, Dereck, if you read carefully. If I were you, and I wanted a lead, I'd take the line that they're in the clear. And then I'd go and see Arthur Coppock."

"I've just come from his block of flats, but he has already gone out. His car's not in the park under the building, the caretaker told me, so he has driven off somewhere. But thanks for the tip, all the same. I'll keep after him."

"I'll join you tomorrow," she promised. "But today Henry and I are on holiday."

So they spent all the morning sunbathing on the beach, which was now much more crowded, and smelling of suntan oil and seaweed and orange peel. They sucked ice-cream cones which Henry bought from the man in a white coat who wandered along the beach with a tray of them. At mid-day, Henry went for another swim, but Kate declared lazily that she couldn't be bothered. When he got back, she had made friends with a black mongrel dog, for which she was tossing pebbles to be raced after and retrieved, and laid at her feet with an excited bark. Kate tired of the game long before the dog did. The dog therefore made so much protesting noise that they decided to leave the beach to him. They dressed, and wandered off to choose a seafront pub at which to get lunch. The Frigate looked the most enticing—not scrupulously clean, but with a small terrace in front, and tables under sun-faded coloured umbrellas recommending soft drinks. Henry said he preferred beer, and got himself a pint, and a gingerbeer shandy for Kate, and two plates heaped with fish and chips. They were consuming these happily when Dereck Andrews passed by.

"Having a nice holiday?"

"Yes, thank you, Dereck. Wish you were here."

"I'm making some progress with The Innocence of Philip Sutton," he confided. "I managed to get a few quiet minutes with Mrs. Grossman, and she proved quite helpful and pleasant. By the way, I think you may be wrong, Kate, about that row in Smith's between Grossman and Sutton. Our man who was checking on it had a talk with the woman in the next room—the guest who complained. She heard quite a lot of it—the loud bits, anyway. Apparently it wasn't about a divorce or a love affair. By what she heard, it was about a money transaction, and one of them was shouting at the other that he'd go to gaol."

"I'll get Butch to look into that," said Kate. "Any luck with Arthur Coppock?"

"No. I think he must have gone somewhere for the day. After all, it is Saturday."

"Gone off with the redhead?"

"In fact, no. I rang her, and she's at home, and doesn't know where Arthur is."

"Golfing, I expect," said Henry, "or something quite ordinary like that."

"Probably," agreed Dereck, moving off. "Have a nice time, you two."

"Sure," said Henry, going into the bar for more beer.

Afterwards a snooze was imperative. They hired a couple of deckchairs under an awning on a terrace off the esplanade, with a view of the children's paddling pool and, beyond, the small lake on which older children were venturing in brightly-coloured pedal-boats. Henry offered Kate a ride in one, but she declined. Not after all that fish, and all those chips. So when the snooze was over, they walked along to the pier and took tickets for the concert party's afternoon performance.

Kate loved all seaside piers; so delightfully silly. She laughed with pleasure at the stalls offering rude post-cards and sticks of rock and candyfloss, and at the enter-tainment hall full of game machines, and a rifle range with plastic ducks wobbling uncertainly along the arti-ficial water, and the ghost train, and the speedboat land-ing-stage, and the old men somnolent beside their fishing lines flung out from the lower deck, and the very grimy café-restaurant, and the curtained booth occupied by the palmist and fortune-teller; though she stoutly refused to have her fortune told, assuring Henry that she always believed it, and it gave her the jim-jams.

The concert party was housed on a small stage in an open-air enclosure of wood-and-glass screens, almost at the very end of the pier. The seats were filling fast, but Henry managed to get a couple in the fourth row. Then the concert. To Kate's delight, they were real pierrots—the men in (somewhat grubby) white costumes, with conical white hats decorated with pom-poms, and the girls in white bodices and fluffy gauze skirts. The show it-self was awful in the best tradition—a remote descendant of the Co-Optimists. The pianist doubled as a light bari-tone who sang sentimental duets with the ageing soprano. The sketches were time-honoured, and the short, stocky comedian so ludicrously unfunny that everybody split with laughter at him.

Kate, as she told Henry, was having an absolutely lovely time and thoroughly enjoying her holiday. During the interval, when Henry had wandered off to try to get cups of tea, she happened to glance at the back of the concert enclosure and noticed a youth standing there, staring towards her. Then she recognized him as Terry Jenkins, the old 'cellist's son. She waved to him, and he started to move uncertainly towards her, but then sud-denly turned and almost ran from the enclosure, out on to the pier.

She spoke of it to Henry when he returned with the two cups of weak tea, much of it slopped into the saucers.

"He looked very odd, Henry—pale and in some sort of distress, as though he were ill. I'm sure he wanted to tell me something, and then lost his nerve and ran. Ought we to try to find him?"

"Tomorrow. Today we're on holiday, remember?"

"Yes, all right," she agreed, but reluctantly. "I hope the boy's not in real trouble. He looked as though he thought he was. Still, as you say, tomorrow . . ."

During the second half of the show they both began to tire of the joke. Henry nudged her and suggested they went on to the next item of their holiday, the boating trip. Kate agreed, and they left quietly, making their way off the pier and along to the little harbour where the fishing boats sheltered, and where Henry had previously noticed that boats were advertised for hire.

They took a sailing dinghy; he no longer felt up to rowing, he said. She was clinker-built, stout, but slow, designed chiefly for tourist fishing expeditions. The man on the hiring quay worried that there was no boatman to take them out, but Henry assured him he was experienced in sailing small craft. The man watched doubtfully, but was obviously satisfied as Henry took her out of the harbour mouth.

Henry took it leisurely. The breeze was south-easterly and weak.

"If we run her out as far as the western headland," he told Kate, "it'll take a couple of hours to tack back."

"Never mind, darling," she replied, settling as comfortably as she could on a hard cushion on the stern sheets and wedging her back against a thwart, "we've plenty of time before dinner. And let's try to find that little Italian restaurant Arthur Coppock mentioned, which he said wasn't too crumby."

"Anything rather than the Royal Albert's Saturday-night dinner-dance, black tie optional," he agreed. "Talking of Arthur Coppock, I wonder if Dereck caught up with him, and got anything out of him."

"Let's talk about him," said Kate. "We've nothing else to do while you hold on this course. And I reckon I'd like to clear my mind a bit about the managing director."

Henry started listing the things they had already said about Coppock. More than anyone else, he had opportunity to put that bomb under Grossman's desk. He could go anywhere in the factory without question or comment. He had keys to everything there.

"But how about the hoaxes?" put in Kate.

Henry begged her to leave that question for the moment. He had established that Coppock had opportunity. There was the additional point that he had been ten minutes late arriving at the factory on the vital morning —most unusually for him. That could be accounted for if he had stopped at a phone booth on his way from home, to muffle his voice and phone the warning about the bomb in the factory.

"I don't say he did," Henry impressed on her. "What I say is that he could have done, and it would fit."

"It still doesn't make sense of the earlier hoaxes."

Again Henry asked her not to press that point just yet. For the next question was, had Coppock sufficient motive to murder Grossman?

"Sex, greed or secrets," Kate reminded him.

"Not sex. The redheaded Vera takes care of that. And, I think, not secrets. We haven't any evidence either way, but we now know that the research was on neutralizing boobytraps. I can't really see that as something a foreign Power would be desperately anxious to get hold of. Nor have we any indication that Coppock either held that sort of political view, or needed the usually somewhat meagre rewards of espionage. I say, not secrets."

"Which leaves greed."

"Exactly. I don't believe that the company was in any sort of financial trouble, or that Coppock had been cooking the books and Grossman discovered it. Grossman Electronics, after all, isn't a small grocery store. It's a sizeable private company, quite large enough to contemplate putting its shares on the public market. It must have accounting staff, probably an accountant as company secretary. Even the managing director could scarcely cook the books of that sort of concern, and, if he did, the murder of any individual, even of the chairman, wouldn't suffice to cover up. So I'm sure it wasn't that sort of motive."

"Are you dismissing Arthur from the court without a stain on his character?" asked Kate.

"Not at all. For there's what we know from Helga. She had pledged her shares to Coppock, some years ago, for the very inadequate sum of £10,000 in cash, which she needed for her delinquent son, George. Part of the deal was that she would pay him usurious interest, and she gave him an option to buy her shares at a very low price at any time he said so. An unpleasant man, Mr. Arthur Coppock, when you take a good look at him."

"But how is any of that a motive for murdering Carl Grossman?"

"On the face of it, it isn't," Henry admitted. "And yet I have a sort of feeling that, somehow or other . . . Helga thought at first that the phone call threatening her was made by Coppock, but then said that it couldn't have been, for certain reasons—and she wouldn't tell me the reasons. What reasons? What could they have been?"

"Search me," answered Kate, turning her head to scan the water. "I say, we're getting near the headland, Henry, and the tide seems to be running out quite fast, and there are a lot of rocks showing up. Do you think we ought to go on?"

Henry took a quick look. "We're all right for a while. I'll turn back soon."

He fell into silence, and there was only the lapping of the sea against the bows, and the gentle slap of a stay. Then he mused, almost to himself, "There was one thing that puzzled me towards the end of my second interview with Mrs. Helga, and still does. I said something which seemed to enrage her—real rage, even though she suppressed it. It showed in her eyes. And I couldn't imagine how my remarks could possibly have angered her."

"Do you remember what you said?"

"More or less. She had just confessed to me about the option she had given to Coppock to purchase, at a low price, her shares in Grossman Electronics which she had pledged to him, to raise that £10,000. Then she asked whether she could contest Carl Grossman's will that left everything to Stella. I said she could, but it would probably be a long legal battle. But if she won, then Carl Grossman's shareholding would go to her." He sat up suddenly. "That's it. Kate, I think I've got it."

"In simple terms," she begged, "for a female."

"That option she had given him to purchase her shares —it must have been worded so that it applied to all the shares she ever held in Grossman Electronics. It never occurred to her, of course, when she signed the option, that anything was in question except her own shareholding at that time. And at that time it was still quite a small concern. As your business editor said, it's only in the past few years that it has expanded in a big way. So then she suddenly realized—and hence the rage—that if Carl Grossman's will leaving everything to Stella could not be found, and he was deemed to have died intestate, all his shares—after death duties, of course—would go to her, his legal wife. And Coppock would hold an option to buy them from her at a ridiculously low price. All he had to do was wait until probate was granted to her, and then exercise his option. He'd damn nearly own the whole outfit, and she would be cheated out of a large fortune."

"Greed."

"Exactly. A fantastic motive. Then there's the will business. Of course Grossman's will in favour of Stella can't be found. Grossman must have entrusted it to Coppock, as he said he did. Obviously there was no written note about it. So all Coppock had to do, once Carl was dead, was to hide the Stella will—or, probably, destroy it. The best assumption that could be made would be that it was in Grossman's desk and was burned in the explosion. But nobody could prove that he had ever executed the will, or, if he had, could say whether it was in the same terms as his solicitors had drawn. So Carl would be deemed intestate, Helga would get his shareholding—and quietly, a little later on, Coppock would exercise his option to buy her out cheap."

"Surely she could show him up."

"Maybe not. Maybe she wanted that £10,000 for something that, if it were known, would implicate her son in a crime. Even if she did expose him, it wouldn't alter his right to buy her shares."

Kate asked hopefully, "Can we challenge Arthur Coppock with all this?"

Henry shook his head. "The only possible thing is to go straight to Roger Wake. Sorry, darling, but this isn't for a newspaper, you must see that."

"I suppose so," she agreed, but slightly disconsolate.

Henry started to turn the boat into the wind for the homeward journey.

As he did so, Kate suddenly called, "Wait a minute, Henry, hold on. I think there's a swimmer in difficulties among those rocks off the headland.

He raised himself to look. "Where? I can't see anyone."

"Slightly over to the right. Wait until the swell comes in."

Henry watched. Then he cried, "You're right. There is somebody there."

He was already bringing the boat round again on the westward course, calling to Kate to scramble into the bows and watch for submerged rocks. She steered him away from three or four as they approached the rocks jutting out from the headland itself.

As they rounded the largest, she cried aloud. For it was not a swimmer, but a corpse, caught among the rocks and exposed by the receding tide, succeeding waves raising and lowering it into and out of view.

Henry manoeuvred alongside as quickly as he could, then thrust the tiller into Kate's hands, telling her to hold steady.

He leaned over the gunwale and tried to free the body. It was a man in fawn-coloured slacks and a white shirt. Across the back of his head ran a dreadful gash, the skull smashed in.

At last he loosened the body from the rocks, and turned it over in the water.

Kate let go the tiller and crawled across the boat to look, then caught her breath.

"You were wrong about Arthur Coppock, Henry," she said unsteadily.

"This is Coppock?"

She nodded, hastily turning her gaze away from the body and looking up at the tall cliff rising from the rocks.

"But perhaps you weren't wrong," she said. "Perhaps the police were getting too close, so he chose suicide."

"I doubt it," said Henry. "There's a huge hole in the back of his skull. It might have been caused by the fall on the rocks. But I'll bet the autopsy shows it was done well before he was in the water."

"You mean he was murdered?"

Henry assented. "In our reasoning about him," he said, "we ignored the vital factor."

"The hoaxer?"

"Exactly. According to Sutton, Coppock had told Grossman he was fairly sure who the hoaxer was. The obvious implication is that, when Grossman was killed, Coppock was pretty certain who the murderer was. There must have been some reason why he didn't tell the police immediately. Perhaps he wasn't sure enough. Perhaps he needed one more piece of evidence, and perhaps he had just found it—so Coppock had to be silenced."

"Then who?"

"I no longer have the slightest idea," said Henry. "And nor have you, I think. And nor will Detective Chief Superintendent Roger Wake have, when we get this back to him."

"We? Oh, Henry, do we have to?"

"Pass me that length of rope. We'll take him in tow."

"Delightful sort of holiday," she muttered, "this turned out to be."

CHAPTER 15

As they entered the harbour mouth, Henry told Kate to clear off when they got ashore. He would see to all the business of fetching the police, making a statement, all that. He told her to go back to the hotel and rest; she looked as though she needed it. Kate, feeling rather sick, consented.

By the time they got to the landing-stage a curious crowd was gathering. Henry got her on to the quay and into the boat-hire kiosk where, mercifully, there was a phone. She was all right now, she told him. She would call the police. Let him get back to the boat, where the attendant and a couple of other men were already lifting Arthur Coppock's body from the water, laying it down on the quay, covering it with tarpaulin.

After she had called the police she rang for a taxi. The police car came almost at once, Kippis hurrying down the stone steps with a sergeant. He did not see her in the kiosk. She saw Henry talking to him. Then her taxi arrived. She was glad to get away.

As the taxi drew up at the Royal Albert, Dereck Andrews was coming down the steps. Looking round to see that he was alone, she told him quietly, "I've a good lead for you. Get down to the harbour, where they hire out the boats. Don't ask questions, just go quickly, or you'll be too late. Henry's there. Take this taxi."

With a gesture of thanks he got in and drove off.

In the hotel lobby Kate paused; an idea came to her. She told the hall porter to ring for another taxi. The idea was that there was somebody it might be worth getting to at once, before the news broke. When the taxi arrived, she gave the driver Vera Sanderson's address.

The girl was sitting in a deckchair in the garden, in the shade of the apple tree. Through one of the windows Kate could see the mother moving about inside the house. She hoped she would stay there.

Vera was startled to see her. "Has something happened?"

"Bad news, I'm afraid."

"Arthur?" she asked sharply. Had she said that rather too quickly? Kate wondered. Had she been expecting bad news about Arthur Coppock? But no, it was natural enough. About whom else would Kate have come to her with bad news?

"I'm afraid so. It's very bad news indeed. Henry and I went out in a boat. We found him in the sea."

The girl was staring at her in horror, stupefied. There was no doubt now that she had expected nothing of this. At last she managed to ask, "Drowned? Arthur drowned?"

"Perhaps."

"What do you mean?"

Kate said, as gently as she could, "You'd better know. He had fallen down the western cliff on to the rocks and into the sea."

Vera put her hands to her mouth, bewildered. She ought to weep, Kate thought. If only she would weep! But she was holding herself in.

"How did it happen? Tell me."

"I don't know. I left Henry to deal with the police, and find out. I couldn't face it."

"Why should he fall from the cliff?" Vera persisted. "What was he doing there?" Then, startled, after a pause, "You're not trying to say that he killed himself?"

"I don't think one can possibly know until after the proper investigation—and that's up to the police. That will tell what happened."

Suddenly the girl dropped her head into her hands. She was weeping now. Kate knelt on the grass beside her chair, touched her arm. For a moment she stiffened, then clutched at Kate's shoulders, pressed her face against her, sobbing, shuddering.

They were like that for a while, Kate silent. Gradually the sobs diminished. At last Vera raised her head, sat back in the chair.

"Thank you," she said.

Kate smiled gently. "I broke all newspaper ethical codes, coming here to tell you."

"Why did you come?"

"Partly because I thought you'd rather have the news from another woman than from a policeman, and partly because I think you ought to be prepared for what I guess may be going to happen."

Vera looked puzzled, not understanding.

"My guess," said Kate, "is that Arthur's death was neither accident nor suicide."

"So what . . . ?"

"I think he was killed."

"Killed? But why?" the girl cried in distress. "Why?"

"I think he was killed by whoever murdered Carl Grossman, because Arthur knew too much, or more likely had just found out something. So he had to be silenced."

Although she was still in shock, Vera had partial control of herself now. She was staring at Kate, with conscious effort. But her eyes were hardening.

"He *had* just found out something. He told me, because it was troubling him. But . . ."

"But what?"

"He didn't think it had anything to do with Mr. Grossman's murder. It couldn't have. Or could it? It was about Philip Sutton."

Kate said quietly, "Would you like to tell me what Arthur had discovered?"

"I don't know the details. Philip had been swindling Mr. Grossman out of quite a lot of money. It had nothing to do with the firm. He had been taking it out of Mr. Grossman's private banking accounts, by getting him to sign papers that he told him were business matters. In some way, this transferred money from Mr. Grossman's bank to various accounts that Philip himself, using business names, had set up in other banks. Arthur gathered it had been going on for a long time. Mr. Grossman was terribly careless about business matters. It never occurred to him to question the papers that Philip put on his desk for signature. I doubt if he even read most of them. And since it was a question of his personal banking accounts, there was no check by the firm's accountants. But then his bank manager got anxious and informed Mr. Grossman privately that something seemed to be wrong. Arthur thought that he must have challenged Philip with it, and that's what the row was about."

"Philip says it was because Carl Grossman wouldn't divorce Stella so that he could marry her."

Vera shook her head impatiently. "That was nonsense. We had all known for a long time there was something going on between Philip and Stella, and so, I'm sure, had Mr. Grossman. Philip didn't want any divorce. He didn't want to marry her. He doesn't really want women. He's a bit queer—did you know?"

Kate nodded. Yes, she did know. She asked how Arthur had known about the swindle.

"Mr. Grossman left some papers in his car when he returned to the works on Tuesday. Somebody put them into Arthur's office, and in the confusion that followed the bombing they were forgotten. A couple of days ago Arthur came across them, and, when he read them, realized what was implied."

"Did he challenge Philip with it?"

"I don't know. He hadn't up to the day before yesterday. That was when he told me about it. He was worrying whether to tackle Philip or not. The trouble was, Arthur said, that he doubted whether a charge could be brought, now that Mr. Grossman is dead. Nobody could prove that the payments were not being made with his consent."

"What for?" asked Kate. And then, when the girl was silent, "Oh, I see. That would be unpleasant, specially for Stella. Did Arthur tell her of it?"

"No. He told nobody except me. He was inclined to go to the police, but wondered whether it would be better to face Philip with it first."

Kate wondered to herself whether he had.

"One thing's important," she advised Vera. "Don't let anybody know that Arthur spoke to you about it, or that you have any knowledge of it—anybody, that is, except the police. You must tell Roger Wake straight away, but nobody else."

Vera seemed puzzled. "Why not?"

"Surely you understand what all this implies. If the row in London was really about this, perhaps Carl Grossman threatened Philip with prosecution, prison even. I did hear from a reporter that a quarrel was overheard about going to gaol. So Philip returned to the factory—one could surmise—and rigged up the boobytrap under Carl Grossman's desk. He couldn't have known there were any papers in Carl's car that could still implicate him—until, perhaps, Arthur told him so. And Arthur is dead. It could be that it's a dangerous thing to know. So don't tell anybody, except the police, that you also know. Just prudence."

Vera was staring at her, starting to shiver.

"Come," said Kate, helping her up, "let's go into the house and phone Roger Wake now."

When Kate got back to the Royal Albert, Henry had already taken a bath and was dressing. She told him where she had been and put the theory to him about Philip Sutton.

Henry paused in the middle of tying his necktie, pondered, then finished the knot.

"It won't do, Kate. The hoaxes. They can only mean a long-premeditated murder. They started a month or more before the row between Grossman and Sutton in London last Sunday night, and presumably before

Grossman had been alerted by his bank manager to what was going on."

"Those damned hoaxes get in the way every time," Kate grumbled.

"I said from the start, they're the key. When we find out why, we shall probably know who."

He told her what had happened with the police. Kippis had been quite forthcoming. There would be an immediate autopsy on Coppock's body. A forensic medical team was on its way from London. But, after a glance at the injury to the skull, Kippis himself felt reasonably certain it was murder. Henry asked if he saw a link with Grossman's death. The inspector shrugged and said that clearly there must be one, though he couldn't say that, so far, he saw it. Henry had gone back to the station in a police car, to make a statement. Kippis said he would ask for one from Kate some time later—not much more than a formality, since Henry could tell him all they both knew.

While he was at the station, a report came in from the car that had gone to the headland. Coppock's car was there, parked against a hedgerow. No attention had been paid to it, for there were several cars parked nearby. It was a favourite spot for holidaymakers to take picnics, or to leave their cars while they walked the clifftop footpath. The car was being brought back for expert examination, but the officer who had found it could see nothing in it to suggest a struggle. But the boot was locked, and there were no keys in the car. Kippis had quickly sent to check whether the car keys were among the things found in the pockets of the trousers Coppock's body was wearing. They were not.

Henry was still there when the preliminary report came through from Coppock's flat. There were no signs of a forced entry, or of a struggle. The caretaker of the block opened the flat door with his pass key. The table on the balcony was laid with the remains of a meal for one person. There was a decanter of wine, but only one glass beside it. A little of the wine was still in the bottom of the glass. There were no lights burning. Coppock's bed had not been slept in. The kitchen and the bathroom were both clean and tidy. The police photographers and fingerprint men were just arriving. Kippis sent back a message that he himself would be there in a few minutes' time.

"The pity of it is, the Sundays will have all this," complained Kate.

"But they'll be bound to say that we discovered the body, and you can come in on Monday morning with your first-hand account."

"It's a slight consolation. Anyway, I've already got my personal and private letter-bomb to lead with. If Sam Kippis does me dirt about that . . ."

"He won't," Henry assured her. "And there's one other thing, most important. Just before I left the station I was asked to step through for a word with the chief superintendent. He had just returned from interviewing Vera Sanderson, who had presumably told him what she told you."

"It expect so. I took good care to get away before he arrived."

"Wake wants an undertaking that you won't use anything you learned from Vera, and won't repeat it to anybody else."

"That makes me cross," Kate declared, reaching for the phone and getting through to the police station. "Chief Superintendent Wake, please. Kate Theobald here . . . Hallo, Mr. Wake. I got your message from Henry. Of course I won't repeat what she told me—except to Henry. As for using it in the *Post*, you really might credit me with a slight sense of responsibility. I would remind you that it was I who told Vera she must get in touch with you at once and say nothing to anybody else. I don't go about deliberately endangering people's lives . . . Well, thank you. Apology accepted."

All day Sunday the police were refusing to disclose the results of the medical examination of Coppock's body, or to say whether they were treating it as a case of murder. Roger Wake was somewhere out of sight, and Sam Kippis declined to yield to the pressure reporters were exerting on him all morning. He merely repeated that, at that stage, there was nothing to say.

He was simply inviting wild speculation in the newspapers, somebody assured him.

Kippis replied that that was the newspapers' concern, not his. "It's no good, boys. We're not talking, and that's flat." He laughed his jolly laugh. "You'd better ask Mrs. Theobald. She always knows more than we do."

Kate made a face at him, and he laughed again and went away. So the newspaper cars turned about, and the men crowded into the Oliver Twist bar. At any rate, Kate murmured to Henry, they could interview each other. The most dramatic stories usually emerged that way.

She saw Geoff Hayward coming in, and motioned to him to step into the lobby.

"Isn't this the wrong bar, Geoff?" she asked. "Shouldn't we be in the snug at the Fishermen's Rest?"

"On Sunday? I doubt if Bob'll be there. He was on duty last night, so I expect he has gone home now. He lives at the back of the town, and uses a little pub in that district, the Duke of Wellington."

"So much the better. Wander out by yourself, Geoff. Wait for me. I'll even trust myself in your car. Henry, darling, can you find something to occupy you for an hour or so? I may not be back for lunch."

"I saw Bill Joseph at the far end of the bar. I'll have a drink with him, and grab a sandwich."

The Duke of Wellington occupied the corner of one of several terraces of small houses, for which it was obviously the local. The regulars, in open-neck shirts and slacks, several of them with their panting dogs on leash, were already turning into the pub, although it had been open for only ten minutes. The public bar was nearly full, but there were only a few people in the saloon. Kate was relieved to see Sergeant Pace's waxed moustaches at the far end of the bar. The sergeant, talking with a couple of cronies, was in his relaxing, Sunday clothes—blue jeans and a somewhat gaudy T-shirt. He greeted them with dignity and inquired what they would drink; in his local pub, Kate understood, he must be allowed to buy the first round. She made hers a shandy.

The sergeant was clearly gratified to be able to introduce to his cronies Kate Theobald of the *Post*, who had found Mr. Coppock's body. The cronies were suitably impressed and, of course, careful not to appear so. They eased, however, when Geoff bought the next round, and he contrived to get them into a group farther along the bar, giving Kate a chance alone with Sergeant Pace.

She asked him what the autopsy had shown. It was murder all right, the sergeant confided. There were two injuries to the back of the head, a contusion as well as the wound that had smashed the skull. The medical chaps were certain that the briuse had been given at least an hour before the heavier blow, and the skull had been smashed for an appreciable time—though probably only short—before the wound was immersed in salt water.

So what, asked Kate, were the deductions?

"Well, it's possible that the skull was smashed by a fall on to a rock at the foot of the cliff before the tide rose and covered it. But, in view of the contusion, it isn't thought likely. What is thought is that the victim was struck down somewhere—possibly in his own flat, though that can't be determined—causing the bruise on the back of his head and knocking him unconscious. Then he was carried in the boot of his car to the clifftop. There are traces on the floor of the boot of human sweat and saliva."

Kate asked if there was any indication of when all this happened.

"It must have been after dark," said the sergeant. "It is thought that the victim was removed from the boot, up there on the clifftop, and his head was stove in with a rock, or perhaps a car spanner, or a tyre lever, before being tipped over the edge of the cliff on to the rocks below. High tide was just after 1 a.m., and by then the rocks would have been submerged to a depth of about two feet. At low tide this morning there was a search along the foot of the cliff, to try to find the weapon. But nothing was found. Of course, it could have been done with a rock which was then thrown over into the sea."

"No witnesses, I suppose?"

"None that we've found yet. There's going to be an appeal on the local radio and the district television, for anybody who was up there on Friday night to go to the police. But since it's usually for a spot of adultery, people aren't all that keen to come forward."

"Any indication in Arthur Coppock's flat?"

"The scientific reports aren't all in yet. But I don't know of anything, except the dinner table. Mr. Theobald told you about that, I expect. It looked as though Mr. Coppock had eaten a meal alone on the balcony, and drunk his coffee, and perhaps another glass of wine, when he was interrupted either by a visitor he let into the flat, or by something—a phone call, say—that made him go out immediately, without clearing away the dishes. But that's all guesswork."

He hesitated, and Kate thought he was going to tell her something else. But then he took a swig of his beer and remained silent, though looking a little awkward.

Geoff could no longer hold off the cronies. He bought another round. Then Kate realized the sergeant was trying to attract his attention on the quiet. So she engaged the cronies in a spirited recital of the thrills of reporting murder. Geoff and the sergeant had a muttered talk together a few paces away.

When they were driving back to the hotel, she asked, "Well, what did the sergeant tell you that he wouldn't tell me?"

"Two things, both almost unbelievable. The first is that Coppock was beaten up in an unpleasant way before he was killed. The medical chaps have established that."

"In what sort of unpleaseant way?"

Geoff looked as awkward as the sergeant had seemed. "It's why Bob Pace didn't like to tell you."

"Come one, Geoff, out with it."

"His hands were tied—there were slight marks still round the wrists—and possibly his ankles too. But the ankles not together. He was beaten and kicked in his, er, private parts."

"Kicked in the balls?"

"Well, yes. Bob Pace felt he couldn't very well tell a woman that."

"It shows a nice sense of delicacy," mumured Kate.

Tortured before he was killed. But why, for heaven's sake?

"The other thing Bob told me,' Geoff went on, "is much more important. He didn't tell you, because he wasn't sure you'd promise not to use it until he gave the all-clear. I promised for you. Hope that was all right."

"That depends on what it is."

"There's one hell of a flap on with the police. About ten miles inland from here a big new hospital has been built for mental cases—psychiatric, they call it, of course. The Queen's driving down tomorrow to open it. It's a long-standing engagement. It was announced a month or two ago."

"So?"

"So there has been a phone call to the police, to say that the IRA are going to attempt an assassination some-where along the country route."

"A hoax?"

"They hope so. But, of course, they dare not risk it. Special Branch men are already here from London. Police are to be drafted in from other districts, to rein-force our lot. There are ten miles of country lanes on the route, much of it through woodland. They'll have to cover every inch of it. Was I right to promise you wouldn't use it? It has to be secret."

'Yes. But I must warn Butch. Oh, it's quite all right, Geoff. He's to be trusted. He won't let it out to anyone. But he must be ready to cover, just in case it isn't a hoax.

I expect he'll get a staff man on the ceremony, instead of a local. Sorry, no offence. Anyway, it certainly can't be you, or me. We've got all we can handle here.'

She broke off, fell silent, preoccupied. She was wondering for what possible reason Philip Sutton should have tortured Arthur Coppock before he killed him.

CHAPTER 16

When the phone rang on Monday morning, just as the Theobalds had finished breakfast, Kate took it. To her surprise, it was Stella Grossman.

"Philip just phoned me from his digs. He asked me to get in touch with you straight away. The police were there, asking him to go to the station to answer some questions the superintendent wanted to clear up. He seemed very agitated. He said you had promised to help him, and please do something." She laughted shortly, bitterly. "He has a great opinion of you, Mrs. Theobald."

Kate asked abruptly. "Did he tell you what it was about?"

"No. What would it be about except the bomb in the factory? And he has answered all those questions several times already." She sounded puzzled.

"Where are you, Mrs. Grossman?"

"At home, of course."

"Stay there, and I'll come out to you as soon as I can. There are developments you ought to know about."

To Henry, who was still in his bath, she called, "I'm taking the car. Okay? I'm going to Warnham Court. That was Stella on the phone."

"Okay," he responded. "By the way, I forgot to tell you her good news. Bill Joseph told me when we had a drink together yesterday. Carl Grossman's will, leaving his shares to Stella, has turned up."

"Where was it?"

"In a locked filing cabinet in Arthur Coppock's flat." Henry emerged from the bathroom. "We were right, darling. Coppock had hidden the will, and pretended not to know anything about it, so that Helga would get the shares, which he could then filch from her. But now, unless Helga contests the will successfully—which she might—Stella's in the money."

"I'll tell her."

"Don't bother. Bill Joseph is bound to have told her already."

As Kate drove out to Warnham Court there fell, for the first time since she had arrived at Loxham Bay, a light shower of rain. It freshened the approach wonderfully, washed the dark green shades of the rhododendrons, the brilliant blues of the hydrangeas, the paleness of the huge circle of gravel, and the circular bed of scarlet and pink roses at its centre. The bed, like the shrubberies, was meticulously weeded. The man who had spoken to her must be a devoted gardener. She wondered whether Stella Grossman managed this great old house on just one gardener, and some sort of help indoors; she had seen nobody. But when she parked Henry's car on the edge of the circle, and rang at the door, it was opened by an old woman in an apron. Somebody, at least. Mrs. Grossman, she said, was expecting her. Mrs. Grossman was in the morning-room.

For that house it was a small, comfortable room; a few easy chairs, a circular library table with tooled red-leather top, a scattering of books on the wall-shelves, a couple of light landscapes in pale golden frames, curtains patterned with yellow flowers, and the morning sun, now dispersing the rain clouds, filtering through the tall, white-painted sash window.

Stella Grossman was seated in one of the easy chairs, with that morning's *Post* on her knees. She waved Kate into a chair opposite. "Good of you to come."

Now that she was not hidden behind sun-glasses, the exquisiteness of the woman was emphatic. She had the colouring of an Irish beauty—dark hair, pale skin, wide blue eyes. Kate felt ordinary beside her, clumsy. And yet, without the shield of the sun-glasses, Stella looked almost pitiful. Until then Kate had thought her lovely but a bitch. Now she felt compassion for her. She was scared. Kate wondered what she was scared of.

"I said I'd help if I could."

Stella glanced at her uneasily. "I don't see how you can. But Philip seems so sure of you." She laughed—that short, bitter laugh again. "He thinks you'll outwit the police and reveal the identity of the real murderer, so that he can gratefully embrace you to a background of violins."

Kate smiled in reply. "Afraid not. But I haven't the slightest doubt that Roger Wake will find the person who killed your husband. He's a remarkably efficient policeman—cold, quiet, methodical, and absolutely brilliant. If Philip's guilty, Wake will eventually prove it. If he's not, then his strongest ally isn't me, it's Detective Chief Superintendent Roger Wake."

Stella's hands were moving nervously on the edge of the newspaper on her lap. Her hands gave away more of her emotions than her face, even with the eyes unshaded, Kate thought.

"Then why has he taken him to the police station to ask the same questions all over again?"

Kate chose her words carefully. "Not the same questions, I think."

"You said there were developments. Please tell me." Stella spoke in a calm voice, but the tension still showed in her hands, and now a little in her eyes.

"You're not going to like this," Kate warned.

Stella shook her head impatiently. "Tell me."

"For some time—a couple of years perhaps—Philip has been working a swindle on your husband's private banking accounts. I don't know the details of it."

"How do you know of it at all?"

"I can't tell you that. You must simply believe me. I gather that what he was doing was slipping among the letters for signature on your husband's desk various papers that transferred sums from his private bank accounts into several accounts that Philip had opened, under fake business names, in other banks. Not long ago your husband's bank manager became uneasy and sent him a warning letter. The sums involved were quite large, totalling several thousand pounds."

Stella was looking tired, strained. "So Philip is not honest," she said quietly. "I never thought that he was. I accept him as he is. How did it become known? Carl faced him with it?"

"When they were in London. It's probably what the quarrel in the hotel was about."

"It was about me—Philip and me."

"A reporter interviewed the hotel guest in the next room, who had complained about the noise. She said she heard shouts about some sort of financial transaction, and threats that somebody would go to prison. I'm afraid I don't believe Philip's story that your husband wanted him to give you up and return to him. I doubt if your husband wanted him back, after what he had seen in the summerhouse. And I'm pretty sure that, given the chance, Philip would have agreed to ditch you."

Kate paused. Stella was absolutely still, and there was no longer any expression in her eyes.

"I think you know, don't you," Kate went on, "that Philip didn't really want a divorce, and that he's not very interested in you, or any woman—but very interested indeed in money."

She added, brutally perhaps, "He'll be devoted to you, now that your husband's will has been found."

Stella still sat in silence, neither assenting nor contradicting. She must have known all along, Kate was sure. Any woman must have known. And she had been trying to hide the knowledge from herhelf, to pretend to herself. But she had to be made to face it, because soon she was going to have to face something a lot worse—Philip and Arthur Coppock.

At last Stella spoke. "Do the police know about this?"

"Some of it."

"Is he to be charged with fraud?"

"I don't know. I'm not sure whether they have found the evidence."

"There is evidence?"

"There was. Perhaps, unless it has now been destroyed, there still is. Your husband had some papers which told the whole thing. He left them in his car last Tuesday morning, when he drove back to the works, just before..."

"Before he was killed."

"The papers were put into Arthur Coppock's office and nobody paid any attention to them. Then, a couple of days ago, Arthur picked them up, read them, and realized what they meant. If those papers still exist, and can be found, I believe the evidence of fraud is there. If they are not found, Philip can say that the payments into his various bank accounts were made by your husband for—well, for something or other."

"For services rendered," said Stella softly.

Kate hurried on. "Arthur decided to face Philip with the papers before going to the police."

"How can you possibly know that?"

"I can't tell you. Please accept that I do know. Then Arthur Coppock was killed. Yes, it was murder."

Stella was staring at her. "So that's what...?"

"I imagine that's what Roger Wake wants to ask Philip about this morning."

"They think he killed Arthur to prevent him from going to them with evidence of a fraud?"

"There have been lesser motives for murder."

"I'm not speaking of a motive," Stella told her. "It was on Friday evening, wasn't it, that Arthur was killed?"

"Yes. Probably just as he was finishing dinner, which he took alone in his flat."

"Philip was with me all that evening—all that night, as it happens."

Kate tried to put this as delicately as she could. "As an alibi, Mrs. Grossman... Well, you are, shall we say, an interested party."

"The alibi doesn't depend on me. All that evening,

from about half past six until well past midnight, we were at a friend's house, with several others present. Then we drove back here."

"Philip never left the friend's house that evening? Not even for an hour?"

"Not even for ten minutes. First we dined, then we made music. Old Oscar Jenkins was there, with one of his girl pupils, who played the viola—played it rather badly. But she made up our quartet."

Kate rose to go. So that was that. Philip Sutton was in the clear over Coppock's death, anyway.

"Then tell him, Mrs. Grossman, that provided he did not kill your husband, he doesn't need my help. If he has to face anything, it will be a charge of fraud, and I doubt if even that can be upheld against him."

"He will, however," said Stella Grossman, not loudly, but grimly, almost harshly, "have to face me."

Kate went out to the car feeling happier because a comparatively pleasant, very lovely women was not, she now guessed, to be snared for her money by a nasty, crooked young poof.

Geoff Hayward was waiting in the lobby when she got back to the Royal Albert.

"You know that the cops picked up Philip Sutton and had him in for questioning this morning?" he asked.

"Yes. Stella phoned me. I've been out there to talk to her. Are they holding Philip?"

"No, he was out of the station in about half an hour. I tried to talk to him, but he wouldn't play. He drove off in the direction of Warnham Court."

"Where, if there's any justice," Kate told him, "he'll get his come-uppance. I think she now understands that he never wanted her, but only the money. I hope she has stopped deluding herself. By the way, do you know what Wake was questioning him about?"

"I can't find out. The police flap has started over the phone threat to the Queen. The Special Branch men are taking it at face value. When anybody talks about a hoax, they simply don't listen. So the county police are covering ten miles of country roads and fanning out through several square miles of woods."

"Big show."

"Sure. Roger Wake is running it from a mobile radio-linked headquarters somewhere on the downs, with the chief constable, who's sweating on his KBE, peering over his shoulder and breathing heavily down his neck. It's probably why Wake cut short his questioning of Philip this morning. This is no day for a mere murder inquiry."

Kate said that she didn't think that was the reason, and she believed she knew what the questioning was about, but she'd like to be sure. Was the worthy Sergeant Pace in the snug?

"No," Geoff replied. "He's holding the fort at the police station. It's why I can't get near him. Bob Pace and a couple of policewomen are about the only strength left in town."

'Ah well, it's not urgent. Come on up to the suite."

Henry was sunning himself on the balcony, sipping coffee.

"Butch phoned," he told her, "with some interesting gossip about George Grossman. Remember you asked him to check at the Yard. That picture Horace took at the church helped to trace him—he was better known to the police as Kenneth Peterson. And it wasn't Australia he went to. It was the Isle of Wight."

"Parkhurst?"

Henry nodded. "He went down with three others for an armed bank robbery in Birmingham five years ago, almost to the day, 14th August. One of the others is still inside. Two have been out for about a year. Kenneth Peterson, alias George Grossman—I suppose it really should be the other way round—came out three weeks ago. Interesting. But I don't see that it helps at all. We already knew he was in with a set of London criminals. It doesn't seem to make much difference to know that he took part in a crime."

"Anything else happened?" asked Kate.

"No, I've just been sitting here in the sunshine. And Kate, I've been going over this whole damn business in my mind."

"Any conclusions?"

"A possible one. I think I may have been wrong."

Kate grinned at him. "I can't believe it."

"Seriously, darling, when you come to test it . . ."

"Test what, Henry?"

"I've been saying all along that the series of hoaxes must have been deliberately planned as a prelude to Carl Grossman's murder. So if we found the hoaxer, we'd have found the murderer. It isn't necessarily so. Suppose the hoaxer really was simply a hoaxer, some idiot doing it for fun. And the murderer realized that this was his opportunity. If he made his murder seem like yet another hoax, it would be taken as part of the series— just as I have taken it, until now. A wonderful red herring."

"Am I beginning to understand?" asked Kate.

"Take an example. If Arthur Coppock hadn't himself been done in, he would have been the most likely. It seems to fit him better than anyone. However, Arthur obviously won't do. So who's your chief suspect now?"

"Philip Sutton."

"Right. Philip quarrelled with Grossman only two days before he was killed. But the hoaxes which apparently led up to the murder began a month earlier, so we've been saying it couldn't be Philip. To suppose he planned it a month before, and it was then sparked off by Grossman's discovery of his frauds, is asking too much of coincidence. But suppose somebody else had been perpetrating the hoaxes. It doesn't matter who. Then, when Philip suddenly knew he must kill Grossman or go to gaol, he realized he could cash in on them. He could make a phone call about a bomb scare that would link the actual bomb with all the earlier false calls."

Geoff Hayward cut in with a question. "Then why hasn't the hoaxer come forward? Anyone would, surely.

Better confess to a lot of silly mischief than risk being suspected of murder."

Henry agreed. "Good point, Geoff. But since he hasn't come forward, there must be a reason."

"Unless you're wrong again," Kate pointed out, "and the hoaxer and the murderer are not two different people, but one and the same."

Henry was concentrating, chewing slowly on one of his knuckles. "Wait a minute. The reason could be that the hoaxer can't prove that he didn't commit the last hoax too, and therefore the murder. So he daren't come forward. He's terrified. What sort of person are we looking for? He must be a weak sort of man, but a man, not a woman. Probably young, stupid, rather vain, badly repressed, thwarted, wanting to feel strong, powerful. And now terrified."

Kate and Geoff said it simultaneously. "Terry Jenkins!"

"Of course," cried Henry. "He was in the factory that weekend. He could have got at the boobytraps somehow. He had enough technical knowledge for the whole thing. No wonder he hasn't confessed to the hoaxes."

Kate was already on the phone, ringing Grossman Electronics, asking for Miss Sanderson.

"And there's another thing," Henry went on, excited. "Whoever killed Grossman must have known that the hoaxer couldn't come forward. He must have known it was Terry. Wasn't there somebody who was thought to have known who the hoaxer was?"

"Yes," said Geoff. "Arthur Coppock."

"Damn!"

Kate was through to Vera Sanderson, telling her that she wanted rather urgently to talk to Terry Jenkins, and was he at the works? Vera replied that he was not. Mrs. Jenkins had phoned earlier in the morning to say that he was not well and she was keeping him in bed for a couple of days, and getting the doctor to him. Kate thanked her and hung up.

"Let's hope Mrs. Jenkins was telling the truth," said

Geoff, "and she isn't covering up because Terry's gone missing and she doesn't know where he is."

"Why should he be missing?" asked Kate, puzzled.

"If Terry turned up dead, and it looked as though he'd committed suicide—found drowned, say—wouldn't that round everything off? Maybe there'd be some clue left to show it was Terry who did the hoaxes. Grossman murder case closed."

Kate was protesting that was wildly fanciful.

"Is it?" asked Henry sharply. "Arthur Coppock may have found something that would identify the man who killed Grossman. And Arthur's dead. And it was obviously meant to look like suicide—but clumsy in execution. Is it so fanciful?"

Kate was making for the door. "Come on."

CHAPTER 17

Henry parked his car round the corner from the terrace in which Jenkins's house stood. Geoff drew up behind. There was no point in making the visit look like a raid. The eyes behind the lace curtains would be busy enough as it was, with three people at Jenkins's door.

The mother answered. "We've nothing to tell you," she declared, making to shut the door again. But Geoff had his foot in it.

"Mrs. Jenkins, this is very important," said Kate gently. "Where is Terry?"

"What business is that of yours?"

"You telephoned the works this morning to say he is unwell and you are keeping him at home. Is he really here?"

"Impertinence!" the woman cried. "Get out of here, or I'll call the police."

The old man appeared in the hallway behind her, asking tremulously what was the matter.

Kate appealed to him. "Mr. Jenkins, your son's safety is involved in this. Is he here?"

"Of course he is," interrupted Mrs. Jenkins. "He's upstairs in bed, and he's not well. Now get out, the lot of you."

"Is that true, Mr. Jenkins?"

The old man nodded. "Yes, he's upstairs."

"May we talk to him? I can't tell you how important this could be."

"Certainly not," the woman blustered. "Clear off."

But the old man stepped forward. "Be quiet a minute, Polly."

She gasped at him and began to mouth again, but he gestured abruptly to her. She retreated a couple of steps, bewildered. He should talk like that more often, thought Kate.

"Why is it important?" Oscar Jenkins asked.

"We think he knows something which he's too frightened to talk about—and he doesn't know how dangerous that could be. For him, Mr. Jenkins."

"He knows nothing about it at all," declared Mrs. Jenkins.

"Be quiet, Polly."

She subsided, her face reddening.

"We want to persuade him to own up to what is no more than mischief, Mr. Jenkins," went on Kate. "I give you my word. We want to make him understand the risk he's running if he doesn't."

The old man stepped aside, restraining his wife with one arm. "Come in, then."

They followed him up the narrow staircase. When his wife made to join in, he told her abruptly to stay where she was. Wonderful, Kate marvelled, how a crisis can bring out unsuspected strength.

Terry was sitting up in bed, in pale mauve pyjamas and dressing-grown. He looked sullen, as usual, and yet, Kate thought, almost relieved.

"This lady wants to ask you some questions," said his father. "Tell her the truth, Terry."

"It's about that bomb, isn't it?" Terry asked defensively.

"Yes, Terry," Kate told him. "Tell me about that."

"I wanted to tell you on Saturday afternoon at the concert party. But then I got scared. I'm very sorry, Mrs. Theobald. I delivered it."

"Delivered it?" she asked, puzzled.

Henry cut in. 'Are you talking about that hoax letter-bomb that my wife got at the hotel?"

The lad nodded.

"Why did you deliver it, Terry?" asked Kate, astonished.

"Mr. Coppock made me. Then he gave me a message to telephone to you from the callbox in the hotel lobby, after I had seen the police leave."

Henry put a chair beside the bed for Kate.

"I think," he told Terry, "you'd better start at the beginning, don't you? Those hoaxes, starting with the one calling the fire brigade on a false alarm to this house—that was you, wasn't it, Terry?"

Again he nodded. He was fixing his gaze on Kate. That, she realized, was to avoid looking at his father. The old man was standing by the window, his face in shadow, silent.

"And the false alarm for the ambulance?" Henry went on evenly. "And the bomb hoax in the cinema? Both you, Terry? And the scare about the poison in the paste at the works? And the railway tunnel?

At each question the boy nodded miserably.

Henry finished off with, "But not the phone call about the bomb that killed Mr. Grossman, eh, Terry?"

"No," he cried, desperate now, jerking upright in bed, pleading, almost weeping. "I swear I had nothing to do with that. Honest. I'm telling you the truth. Nothing. Nothing at all."

Kate soothed him. "All right, Terry. We believe you. But the hoaxes—why did you do it?"

He was sullen again. "I don't know." He glanced towards his father, then quickly back again to Kate. "Everything was going wrong. All the fellows at the works, laughing at me, my clothes and all that. Calling me sissy. And I couldn't get on. Mr. Grossman said he'd help, but then he forgot all about it. Mr. Coppock was holding me back, I know he was. I'm as good at electrical circuits as any of them. The foreman said so. But Mr. Coppock . . . And then there's Millie, jeering at me, and she wouldn't . . ."

"Who's Millie?" asked Kate.

Old Jenkins broke in. "The girl next door. All right,

son, be easy. I've been wondering for a long time if it was you. Now you've got it off your chest, you'll be all right."

"Did anyone know you were pulling these hoaxes?" asked Henry suddenly, sharply.

"Mr. Coppock knew."

"How?"

"When I rang the works about the poison, he recognized my voice. He got me round to his flat and faced me with it. When I admitted it, he just laughed, and said it was all good fun, but I'd better stop, and not do anything more unless he told me. So I did stop."

"The railway tunnel came after the poison hoax," Kate pointed out.

"I'd already done that," muttered Terry, "before Mr. Coppock talked to me. He said that if I did any more, I'd get into awful trouble. And he said I was to do just what he told me to do, or else."

Henry asked, "And did he tell you to do anything more?"

"Only to deliver that parcel to Mrs. Theobald at the hotel, and then make the phone call with the message he gave me on a piece of paper, directly the police had gone."

"Have you still got the paper?"

"Yes, I've still got it."

Kate sat in silence, pondering. It was fairly clear now that Arthur Coppock had planted the bomb that killed his partner. It had to be done that weekend, before Grossman could make a fresh will, otherwise there'd be no chance of Helga inheriting, and Coppock would have lost control of the firm, for which he had planned so carefully and ruthlessly. Probably, she thought, he intended a little later to kill Terry too, and make it seem like suicide. He could have coerced the boy into writing a confession to the hoaxes, so worded that, as a seeming suicide note, it would appear that he was confessing to the murder too. That would have been damn near perfect cover.

The chief mistake Coppock had made was not to

appreciate how damaging would be the probing by newspaper reporters. How unnerving it must have been, Kate realized, to have Geoff and herself actually in his office, by pure chance, when he knew the bomb to kill Grossman must explode in a few minutes. She had an odd, unpleasant recollection of the sweatiness of his palm as he shook hands and tried to get them to go. He had certainly kept his nerve then. But gradually it must have weakened as she and Henry got more and more involved with the Grossman family, and particularly, she supposed, with Terry Jenkins. Terry was the vulnerable point. What an absurd, almost desperate risk the man had taken in using the boy in the ridiculous business of delivering the hoax letter-bomb to Kate herself. Coppock's plan must have been to fake the boy's suicide, or the risk would have been too great for such a careful man to take.

Now the boy was safe, because Coppock was dead. The next question was glaring enough. Who, then, had killed Coppock?

With one exception, everything pointed to Philip Sutton. Coppock had discovered Philip's frauds. Coppock must have challenged him with proof of them. Motive enough, surely.

The exception, of course, was that throughout the evening on which Coppock was killed, Philip was playing in a string quartet. Could that alibi possibly be false? Kate wondered. Could he somehow have faked the assumed time of Coppock's death, made it seem like just after dinner when it was really after midnight? Then only Stella would know. But Kate shook her head at herself. The forensic doctors would never have been deceived about the approximate time of death.

Oscar Jenkins had stepped over to the bed and put his arm round his son's shoulders. "All right, Terry. Now you've owned up, it'll be all right."

"Later on today the police will come round and ask you about all this," Kate told him. "Tell them the truth, all of the truth, every little detail."

"What'll happen to me?" he asked in a quaver.

"You'll be in trouble. What else can you expect? But provided you tell the police everything, the trouble won't be too bad." To Oscar Jenkins she added, "You'll keep him here, won't you, Mr. Jenkins, until the police come?"

The old man nodded. "But you'd better all go now."

She agreed. "And, Mr. Jenkins, don't worry any more about Terry's safety. The risk we feared doesn't exist now."

When they returned to their cars, Kate said they would have to tell Roger Wake as soon as they could.

"Not before this afternoon," said Geoff. "He's still up on the downs, manoeuvring the guard on the Queen's route back from the hospital."

"No particular hurry. And Henry, I take my hat off. You were right."

"The murderer and the hoaxer not the same person," he agreed. "I suppose we're all of the same mind. Arthur Coppock killed Grossman. There doesn't seem any other possibility."

"But who killed Arthur?"

"Heaven knows. I think it must be Philip Sutton. There must be something phoney about his alibi. But that's for the police."

"If Arthur hadn't been killed," said Kate, "I'm sure he was going to kill young Terry, incriminate him somehow as the hoaxer, and the murderer, and fake his suicide."

"Speculation," Henry pointed out, "and now merely academic. All the same, that could have been the idea. Coppock realizes the possibility of the series of hoaxes which he knows Terry is perpetrating, slips his murder into the series, and then the hoaxer is found dead, suicide, a note of confession. It would have been the logical way of using the opportunity of the hoaxes. Complicated, perhaps, and a bit devious. But, as we know from the trap he set for Mrs. Helga, Coppock had that sort of mind."

"How about today's hoax?" asked Geoff Hayward suddenly. "If it is one, that is."

"Today's? You mean the phone call saying there'd be an attempt to assassinate the Queen?"

"If it is a hoax," asked Geoff, "who did it?"

Henry chewed on his knuckle. "Terry again? We should have put that to him."

"I'm sure it wasn't Terry," said Kate. "He'd have told us."

"Then who?" repeated Geoff.

Henry reasoned slowly, "If one man could make use of the opportunity of a series of hoaxes to commit a crime, why shouldn't another man have the same idea?"

"What for?"

"To clear the town of police," suggested Kate. "First time I met Sergeant Pace, Geoff, do you remember? He said it was a good job there was no serious crime in the town, the police were so exhausted by the hoax business. Today, the town's wide open."

"For what?" muttered Henry, almost to himself. "It would have to be robbery, big scale, probably armed. Monday. The banks are full of the weekend money, bundled up for collection by the security trucks."

He and Kate looked at each other inquiringly, then exclaimed together, "George!"

She started guessing swiftly. "He come out of Parkhurst three weeks or so ago. Comes to his mother. The town's in a fever over the hoaxes. George sees the chance —can he find some way of hoaxing the police out of the town for the day! Then he hears of the Queen coming to open the new hospital ten miles off in the country. The engagement had already been publicly announced. That's it. So he whistles up his two pals already out of gaol after the last bank raid . . ."

Henry was pushing her into his car. "You take it, and go straight back to the hotel, and stay there. Promise? You have to, Kate. This could be dangerous."

"What about you two?"

"Geoff'll drive to the police station to warn his friend

the sergeant. There'll be radio contact. If anything starts, the police cars could be back in a quarter of an hour. I'm going with Geoff. There's something I want to check. Don't worry, we'll be well out of harm's way. And so will you, Kate. If we've guessed right, these men are going to be armed. Back to the hotel, and stay there. That's an order, mate."

Geoff started his car. Henry jumped in.

As they made off, Kate complained, "No I know just how Mrs. Jenkins felt, poor soul."

She waited a few minutes, rebellious, contemplating following them. But then she sighed and started the car; better return to the hotel.

She dropped down the hill towards the little harbour, at the eastern end of the esplanade. Traffic was snarled at the road junction, and held her up for several minutes. No policeman on traffic duty, she reflected. The man who should have been there was tramping through the woods ten miles away, keeping a sharp lookout for non-existent terrorists until the Queen's cavalcade had gone by. Meanwhile a large articulated truck, trying to turn sharply on to the harbour road, had stuck itself across the junction.

By now it was middle day, with the sun right overhead and no cloud anywhere. The earlier drift of rain had cleared, the sea was calm and blue. She felt hotter and hotter, stuck in the traffic jam. The car's cooler seemed to make scant difference while it was stationary, and the idling engine was overheating so fast that she switched it off; and the engine heated faster still; so she switched on again and tried a few bursts of revving, to speed the fan; it had almost no effect, and she left the damned thing alone, and undid the top two buttons of her blouse, easing it away from her skin.

Two men from cars farther ahead had got out on to the road now to guide the artic., which was gradually turning at last and pulling clear. This was as well, for some idiot at the rear was beginning to sound his horn, repeatedly, insistently, uselessly; few things more irritat-

ing in a traffic jam on a really hot day. "Shut up, you
fool," she muttered crossly. But then the traffic began
to ease forward and the blare of the horn ceased.

So much traffic had accumulated during the delay,
however, that even when it moved again it was only
crawling along the seafront road. After about a hundred
yards of this, Kate turned off to the right. She had remembered that the town's main shopping street ran par-
allel to the seafront, one block inland. There would be
less traffic there, for it was a no-parking street. The car
park lay just behind it, in a network of narrow, ancient
alleyways, where several old buildings had been razed,
and a morose attendant in a blue overall took parking
fees at the gate. At the far end of the main street she
would be able to turn into the rear approach to the Royal
Albert.

There was more of a block in the shopping street than
she had expected. Only a few cars were travelling along
it, but they were delayed by throngs of pedestrian shop-
pers wandering across the roadway, and by a couple of
vans unloading into two of the biggest shops, a grocery
store and a furnishing house. There was also, she noticed, a small green van drawn up outside the big bank
on the second corner.

The commotion began abruptly. There was sudden
shouting ahead, a woman screaming, a rush of people
tumultuously along the narrow footways. Only by thrust-
ing on her brake did Kate manage to avoid collision with
the car that pulled up short in front of her, without warning. She cursed, peered ahead, then swung the Jag against
the far kerb, jerked open the door, yanked herself out so
that she could see what was happening.

Outside the bank stood a man, crouching forward,
threatening, an automatic rifle poised in his gloved hands.
He was wearing brown overalls. His face was shrouded
by a nylon stocking pulled down over his head beneath a
woolen balaclava. Traversing the gun in a menacing
semi-circle, he was shouting at the crowd, shouting at
them to keep back; the terrified people recoiling, the few

cars pulling into the kerb, one of them trying to back away down the street. The noise was penetrating, the gunman shouting, women screaming, a dog excitedly barking.

At the bank entrance stood another man, similarly dressed, similarly armed, but with his rifle pointing into the interior. A third man, dressed the same, but unarmed, came running out of the bank, hoisting several clumsy sacks. He thrust the sacks into the back of the little van, rushed back inside, emerged with three more sacks, then scrambled into the driving seat, yelling to the two others.

One of the gunmen fired a warning burst into the air, a sharp crackle, and the whine of ricochets.

The bank's alarm bell suddenly started up with a great clangour.

The crowds surged nervously towards the van, then recoiled. The two gunmen were inside now, the rear door slammed behind them, and the van was racing away from the kerb, tearing along the street away from Kate's position.

In a couple of seconds it reached the next corner, where the side road climbed steeply uphill into the town.

Suddenly came a curious sound from the crowd, a great gasp, like a vast intake of breath. For hurtling down the hill of the side road came a rusty old car. Kate clutched her hand to her mouth. Geoff's car.

Before there was time to shout, the old car rammed the side of the van as it turned the corner towards the hill. The van driver swerved violently to avoid it, but failed. The old car rammed it at speed, tore open the side of the van, sent it careering sideways, brakes screeching, engine roaring. The van skidded against the steep kerb, pitched over on its side with a crash, wheels racing, engine still truculent, shatter of glass.

Geoff's car pitched the other way, rolled over twice, slid on its roof with a tearing noise and battered through a plate-glass shop-front, lying half in the window and half out, wheels in the air.

A moment of silence, of disbelief.

Then the crowd surged forward, shouting.

Kate ran with the rest. As she ran, cold with fear, she saw a man scramble out of the back of the green van and run into the network of alleyways behind the main street. Three or four men started after him. But there was a single shot, one of the men spun round, yelling, grasping his left arm. The others abruptly halted, turned to tend him.

Kate ran through the crowd, pushing her way. Her heart was thumping. Henry. Henry.

She came up to Geoff's car. A man was hauling himself out. Geoff. Blood was oozing down his cheek. He moved with difficulty, grateful for the men seizing hold of him, helping him up.

"Geoff," she shouted. "Where's Henry?"

He turned round towards her, startled, then called, "It's all right. I dropped him off on the way. How did you get here?"

She felt weak. She thought she'd drop. But somebody held her up. Inside her brain she was numb with thanks.

Then Geoff was beside her, arm round her.

"It's all right, Kate. Just me in the car. Henry had a call to make, so I dropped him off. But how did you get here?"

"Geoff!" she exclaimed. "It was the bravest thing I ever saw."

He grinned. "Don't give the game away. I couldn't have stopped anyway—not on that hill, with those brakes."

"Geoff, darling. Are you hurt?"

"Cut my face a bit." He moved, and she saw he was limping badly. At her look of dismay he grinned again. "And I haven't half sprained my bloody ankle."

Men of the crowd were around him, touching him, grunting praise, to Geoff's embarrassment. So, with his arm round one man's shoulder, he was limping over towards the van. The crowd around it opened a way for him, awed, respectful.

"What happened here?" he asked.

"There were three of them," a man offered. "One made a run for it. The two others are here, knocked out, seemingly. Maybe the bastards are dead."

One of the men was slung across the driving cabin of the van, the other hanging half out of the rear door, the sacks of money piled on top of him where they had been flung by the impact.

"All the money's here," volunteered someone.

A stout, elderly man in a dark suit was gripping Geoff's arm. "My heavens, that was a great thing, Geoff."

"Hallo, Mr. Coombes. Your money's safe anyway." Geoff turned to Kate. "This is Mr. Coombes, the bank manager. This is Kate Theobald of the *Post*. She'll give you a great write-up."

"You get the headlines, Geoff," the bank manager protested. "Not many would have the guts to do that."

"Too right," Kate agreed.

An ambulance came shrieking up now, the ambulance men running out with stretchers, blankets. They got the two men from the van, pulling off balaclava helmets and stocking masks. One man was muttering, so he was all right. Kate recognized neither of them.

The ambulance crew were examining the other man. They got him on a stretcher, eased him towards the ambulance.

"No, not dead, but pretty bad," one of the orderlies replied to questions from the crowd.

"Serve the bastard right."

Coombes, the bank manager, called after them, "Hang on a minute, you chaps. Here's Mr. Hayward, who rammed the van in his own car. He's hurt too. You should take him."

The ambulance man came back, solicitous. "Sure thing. You want to come along, sir?"

"No," said Geoff cheerfully. "I'm all right. Thanks all the same. No real damage done. Wish I could say the same for Flossie."

He was moving back across the road.

"Flossie?" asked Kate.

"The car. Her name's Flossie." He was gazing down at her in sorrow. "Seventy-five quid she cost me, and a lot of work. And I loved her dearly. And she's a write-off."

"Don't worry about that, Geoff," Coombes assured him. "I promise you that'll be taken care of. There are rewards for recovering stolen money."

"You'd better come in the ambulance, Mr. Hayward," the man was calling after him. "You ought to come to the hospital for a check-over."

Geoff waved back. "No, really, I'm all right. And Mrs. Theobald and I have work to do, eh Kate? Make a pretty damn good story, eh?"

"You bet."

"Mrs. Theobald'll look after me," he called back to the ambulance orderly. "We've got work to do."

The man reluctantly assented and turned back to the ambulance, which drew off.

"Where is Henry?" she asked.

"I dropped him off in Gladstone Street. He wanted to check on something with Mrs. Helga. Then I went on and warned Bob Pace at the police station. He got on the blower to the Superintendent, out in the hills. I reckon quite a few police cars are screaming back towards the town by now."

"Listen, Geoff. You stay here while I get the car. Then we'll go back to the hotel and do the story."

He smiled awkwardly. "I'd like to write my bit myself, Kate, if you don't mind. You put the grammar in."

"You write what you like. All I'll add is the hyperboles and the screamers."

The crowds were starting to disperse as she made her way back along the street. The few cars were moving again. She saw that the bank manager had stationed his commissionaires, and a couple of hefty young clerks, on guard over the spilled van and the sacks of notes.

On her way she caught one snatch of conversation. "Where on earth were the police?" "Lord knows. You'll never see a copper when you need one." "But really, in a thing like this. It's quite disgraceful."

Kate got into the driving seat of her car. She saw that she had left the ignition key in the starter lock. She smiled rather wearily to herself. Not to tell Henry. Henry was fussy about always taking car keys with you.

She started the engine. As she did so, the car door was opened on the other side, and a man slid into the seat beside her.

Kate turned sharply, with annoyance. "What's the idea?"

Then she saw it was George Grossman. In his hand he held a small black pistol. The muzzle touched her ribs.

"Just drive on, Mrs. Theobald," he said quietly, "and don't try anything. Turn right now, this side of the bank, then right again, then out on to the seafront. Then I'll give you directions."

She moved the car off. One glance at the man's face had been enough—taut, drawn, desperate.

CHAPTER 18

Henry had about ten minutes' walk after Geoff had dropped him off.

"Will this do?" Geoff had asked, halfway down the hill. "It's through there, a straight road, not much more than half a mile. I ought to get to the cops as fast as I can."

"Sure," Henry had said, getting out of the car. "No particular hurry for me."

He walked at a leisurely pace, straightening the suspicions in his thoughts. He wondered how much Helga Grossman was likely to know. Some of it she must know, there could be little doubt of that. The answer to one question alone would establish that she knew something. He would put that question to her, and she could scarcely dodge it; to do so would be damning. But whether he could lead her much farther was less sure.

When he reached the house, he at first got no answer to the bell. He rang a second time, and waited; then a third time. In the silence he stepped across the small front garden, but could see little of the interior of the front room through the heavy net curtains at the windows. Anyway, the front room was not that in which she had received him on the two previous visits, and in which he had the impression that she lived. That was at the back, facing on to a small, unkempt garden rising steeply up the hill into a thicket of trees and bushes.

He wondered if he could get round to the back of the house, but the way was blocked by a tall wooden gate, which was locked. So he returned to the front door and rang Mrs. Helga Grossman's bell again, and waited.

He felt certain she was in. He contemplated ringing the bell on the adjoining door; the tenants of the flat above might know if she was in or out. But then Mrs. Grossman's door slowly opened and she stood facing him.

He tried to assess what had changed in her. She stood as firmly upright as ever, grasping the silver handle of her ebony stick. Her face was as calm, as grave. But the skin seemed to have tautened over the angular framework of the skull, as though in a grimace of pain, and her eyes to have faded to a paler blue, underscored with shadow. Yet, curiously, the hint of agony seemed to make her appear younger, more vigorous, as though the act of making some essential decision had revivified her.

"Well?"

"I must talk to you, Mrs. Grossman. May I come in?" She hesitated, so he added, "It is vitally important. It's about your son."

She stared at him for a moment, then turned, without speaking, and slowly led the way along the corridor to the big, dark room at the back of the house where he had been twice before. Without being asked, he took the same seat on the settee, and the woman lowered herself on to the throne-back chair.

"Well?"

"I'm going to be blunt. That document you signed giving Arthur Coppock an option to buy your shares— you've got it back, haven't you?"

Her self-control was remarkable, and so was the speed with which she understood that a denial would not do, and came up with an alternative.

She inclined her head gravely. "Yes. Arthur returned it to me."

"Returned it to you?"

"Through the post. I received it this morning."

"Without explanation?"

"With nothing. Just the document, addressed to me, and marked Personal and Private."

"Then how do you know it was sent by Arthur Coppock?"

"Who else?"

"I don't know. But Coppock was killed on Friday evening. Today is Monday. One would have thought that any letter he posted would have been delivered on Saturday."

She shrugged. "Perhaps he posted it after the last collection on Friday."

It was possible, but Henry thought it highly unlikely. He could advance a more probable theory; but perhaps not quite yet.

"Why do you think Arthur Coppock returned the paper to you, Mrs. Grossman?" he asked.

"Perhaps he did not wish to quarrel with me, now that Carl is dead, and I might inherit control of the company."

"Mrs. Grossman," said Henry quietly, "I think that paper gave Arthur Coppock the right to purchase, not only your existing shareholding in the company, but any other of its shares you might hold at any time. So if you inherited your husband's shares, Coppock could take them from you and control the company himself. So why should he return the paper to you through the post?"

"I am not in court to be questioned by a lawyer," she abruptly answered. "You said you had something important to say to me about my son. Well?"

"A few years ago you told old Mr. Joseph, Bill Joseph's father, then your solicitor, that your son had gone to Australia. That wasn't true. He was serving a prison sentence for armed robbery, from which he was discharged only three weeks ago. I assume you knew all that."

"As his mother, should I not tell a lie, from pride?"

"Of course. And I sympathize with you."

"The money came too late," she murmured, almost to herself, the look of pain deepening in her eyes.

"The £10,000?"

She nodded. "Three days before I got it, he was arrested. If I had had it in time, I could have got him out of the country to safety." She began to glare angrily at Henry. "Everything was arranged. He had obtained a passport in a false name—I do not know how. His travel tickets had been purchased. Ah, you are a lawyer, a prim lawyer. You think it was wrong that I should help him to escape when he had committed a crime."

"A crime of violence," Henry put in quietly.

"Any crime. Say it had been murder. Any crime. He is my son—my son, I tell you, my son. You think I would not help him, no matter what he has done?"

"Even murder, you say?"

"Yes, I say so. Even murder." She broke off, then continued in a sad voice, "But the money came three days too late. If I had had it a few days earlier I could have sent him where he would never have been found."

"Not to Australia," said Henry.

"No, not to Australia."

She looked away from him for the first time since they had sat there.

Henry's thoughts were running. Somewhere George would never have been found? South America? Just possible, though extradition was easier than it used to be. Certainly nowhere else in the West. In the East then? That could be it. Behind the Iron Curtain.

But how could a mere criminal, fleeing from arrest, hope for asylum there? Where in East Europe could he expect to be admitted? East Germany? George, after all, was German by birth.

At that moment Henry hit on it. He could even perceive, in a kind of flash, the outline of how it could be done.

"If you had received the £10,000 a few days earlier, Mrs. Grossman," he softly inquired, "what would you have done with it? Would you have paid it, as instructed, into a somewhat obscure bank in the City of London, into an account already opened in your son's false name —the same as on the passport? I suppose he would then have taken the necessary documents to the place of

refuge. Once he was there, he would have authorized
the money to be paid out, in sterling, to some foreign
trading corporation, which could use it to buy British
goods for export to the country of its origin. And the
man to whom George had fled would be paid an equiva-
lent sum in the currency of his own country. Just for the
moment, I can't remember what the currency is in East
Germany."

Mrs. Grossman was gazing at him again, unflinching,
silent.

"You were to have sent him to his father. That was it,
wasn't it, Mrs. Grossman? Bill Joseph thought you probably had no idea who George's father is. But he's wrong,
isn't he? You were living with an official in Germany during the war, perhaps quite a high official—high enough,
and useful enough, to get himself accepted in East Germany. Quite a lot of Nazis fled there, I've heard, and,
because they were needed, were allowed to cover up their
past."

Henry paused. The woman still said nothing, though
now and then her lips seemed to begin to move.

"But the money came too late, Mrs. Grossman.
George had been arrested three days before, and would
go to a prison term. What did you do with the money? Is
it still in that little bank in the City of London? Is it there
in readiness, in case George again needs to run? Any
crime you said, Mrs. Grossman. Even murder, you said."

At last she spoke, but in little more than a whisper.
"He is my son."

"This time it is murder," said Henry. It had to be said.
"He killed Arthur Coppock. After our last meeting you
told him the whole story. He had not known it before.
I don't think you realized what he would do. If you had,
you would have stopped him. He went round to Coppock's flat that night. Coppock admitted him. Why not?
He had known him from childhood. Then George pulled
a gun on him, tied him up, tortured him until he told him
where the paper was hidden. Perhaps he didn't mean to
kill him. It was not necessary. Coppock could not have

talked. But the blow on the head was heavier than George intended."

"Be quiet," the woman begged. Her stance in the chair had scarcely altered, except that she was leaning slightly forward. She began to tap her cane nervously on the floor. "Be quiet. Be quiet."

Henry had to finish it. "So then George panicked, tried to stage a suicide. Not very convincingly. He may have thought he would get away with it, but you knew he could not. So he must run, and you must help him. Your son."

She was tapping more heavily with her cane. Her voice was rising. "Be quiet, I tell you. Stop. Be still."

"But it won't do. You're intelligent enough to see that. You know that it won't do. So you will come with me to the police . . ."

The door swung open behind him. Henry turned quickly, startled.

"Kate!"

She was standing in the doorway, one arm twisted behind her. In the shadow of the corridor loomed George Grossman.

"He has a gun, Henry," she warned quickly, trying to keep on the calm side of hysteria.

George pushed her farther into the room. She grunted at the extra pain in her arm. Henry jerked up from his chair.

"Don't try anything," the man warned. He was tense, taut strung, clearly desperate.

Now Henry could see the small black pistol held against Kate's side. Henry stood motionless, silent.

"The bank papers," George curtly ordered his mother. "And I must have some money. Cash. It went wrong."

"Let my wife go," said Henry. "We won't interfere."

George laughed brutally. "I'll see to that."

"Listen to sense," urged Kate. "Your bank robbery failed." Aside to Henry: "Geoff rammed their getaway van with his old car. Two of them are in hospital. This man got away. Geoff's all right, not badly hurt. I went to get our car to pick him up, and this man got in beside me with a gun, and made me drive here."

Helga Grossman had risen from her chair and was moving slowly towards the escritoire, stooping to unlock one of the lower drawers.

"A robbery that didn't come off, and you're on the run," said Henry. "Not all that serious. Don't make things much worse for yourself. The hostage idea never works. Let my wife go. We'll not interfere. Lock us up in the cellar here, or anywhere you like, for twenty-four hours. Then your mother can let us out. By then you'll be away. Take my car if you like."

Helga Grossman was lifting a small black leather wallet from the drawer.

"Be sensible," Kate urged George again. "Even if you don't get away, even if you're caught, what is the worst? A bank robbery that failed."

"And murder," said Helga abruptly. "He knows, Georg."

"Murder?" exclaimed Kate, aghast.

"He killed Coppock," Henry told her.

"Oh God!"

The mother was straightening herself, the wallet in her hand. Henry tried desperately to guess what George's getaway plan must be. He expected to have his share of the haul of notes from the bank raid. They must have had stolen cars parked somewhere near. He couldn't have risked Customs, of course, with that lot on him. He had probably hired a cabin cruiser in the next holiday port along the coast to take them all to some remote French beach. A car would be waiting there, the boat would be abandoned. Where would George be making for? Vienna, probably—the easiest route through the Curtain, through to Prague, then to East Germany. His father, alerted in advance, would have appointed somebody to meet him in Vienna, to cache the money safely for collection later, and to get him over the frontier.

And now that the bank robbery had failed, what now?

Helga Grossman had unlocked another drawer in the

escritoire and was fumbling within it for a bundle of notes.

"I have about £200 for emergencies, that's all, Georg."

"Mrs. Grossman," pleaded Kate, "tell him not to make things worse. Tell him to see sense."

What is the plan now? Henry was asking himself repeatedly. What now?

George Grossman himself gave the answer, as though the question had been spoken.

"You go out first," he told Henry. "I follow with your wife. If you try anything, I shoot her. Don't kid yourself. I mean it. What does it matter to me? If I'm caught, it's life anyway. So keep your nose clean. I get in the back of the car with her. You drive. I'll tell you where. And remember, if anything goes wrong . . ."

Henry was guessing desperately. Grossman would have abandoned the idea of getting away in the boat. There would be no need for that, now that there were no banknotes to carry. So he'd make for an airport, Gatwick probably, where he'd buy a ticket for Vienna and take the first plane out; always room for one more passenger. What would happen to Kate and himself?"

Somewhere on the way he would be ordered to pull off on to a lonely side-road. There would be two bodies in a ditch, undiscovered, probably, until George was over the Austrian frontier.

The only chance was to jump him.

Henry tensed himself. There had to be a moment when his mother handed him the wallet and the money, when his attention would waver for a brief span, and the pistol would not—just for that moment—be pointing at Kate.

Helga Grossman was moving slowly over to her son, leaning on her stick. Her face was drawn with grief, with horror.

For one moment Henry thought of a last appeal to her. But useless.

She reached George and was handing him the bundles.

Henry jumped.

George saw him coming, swung the pistol.

"No," shrieked his mother, flinging herself at him.

There were two shots. At the second, Henry knocked the gun from the man's hand. George dived for it, but his mother had clung with her arms round his legs as she sank.

Henry got there first, grabbed the gun, swung round.

George had backed through the door, run for it. A car door slammed.

From the distance came the first howls of the police sirens, swelling rapidly as the cars came racing back into the town.

"He'll never make it," cried Henry.

Kate did not answer. She was kneeling on the floor by the woman, gently easing her on to her back, revealing the scarlet stain soaking across the front of her dark dress and on to the fringe of her thin woollen shawl, and the froth of blood and spittle oozing from her mouth.